Praise for LOVE CHANGES....

"...Love Changes is wonderful, perfect for the beach! When I sit in the sun, I read."
—Nikki Giovanni (via postcard from Aruba)

"Eartha Watts-Hicks has written a touching story that captures the bittersweet, often agonizing, love between generations. A beautiful first novel!"
—Valerie Wilson Wesley, author of Playing My Mother's Blues and the Tamara Hayle Mystery Series

"...they were all stand alone characters that you couldn't help but fall in love with. My favorite character was Mia, by the way...."
—KelliJonee Smith (Reader via Amazon)

"Eartha Watts-Hicks' "Love Changes" was an excellent debut novel. A story containing love, friendships, family, betrayal, lies and forgiveness, "Love Changes" connects with readers. The characters were your average everyday people. The storyline was engrossing. I highly recommend this novel!"
—Reviewed and Rated 5 Stars by LeonaR of Oosa Online Book Club

"Eartha Watts Hicks has written a lovely story about coming of age, delicately fusing deep issues between the pages of this novel, without being preachy...The characters were decent, every day type people – each with their own issues, struggles and decisions to make...Excellent debut!"
—Tumika Patrice Caine (Say What?? Book Club)

Is This The Beginning of The End?

Part III

Eartha Watts Hicks

$\mathcal{F}$or my mother, Renee H.

You are my oldest and dearest friend. Thank you for giving me life, for being my angel in times of trouble, and for teaching me as best you could.

ACKNOWLEDGMENTS

This work was made possible by The Harlem Writers Guild, Project Enterprise, The Center for Black Literature, The Hurston-Wright Foundation, Cultivating Our Sisterhood International Association, Future Executives, Incorporated, The New York City Housing Authority Branch of the NAACP, Union Grove Baptist Church, and Gustavus Adolphus Lutheran Church. A donation of any amount to any of these organizations would further assist in empowering others.

This story was inspired, in part, by the song, "Love Changes." Written by Skip Scarborough, this song was originally released by R&B group "Mother's Finest" in 1978. It was covered and performed by Kashif and Meli'sa Morgan, produced by Kashif in 1987. May he rest in sweet harmony....

We Had Yesterday...

*I*T HAPPENED QUICKLY, BUT WHEN IT WAS OVER, Romell was on the floor. He groaned like I put a serious hurtin' on him. I always knew I had skills. But Romell was solid, all muscle. I'm no slouch, but realistically, I couldn't have hurt him if I tried. Romell was just overreacting, seriously overreacting. We were so close for so long that maybe our attempt to remain platonic was just staving off the inevitable. But, when and if things between us ever did turn sexual, this was also inevitable: something would happen that neither of us would ever forget. Romell just wasn't ready for my reaction. Quite frankly, neither was I.

♥ ♥ ♥ ♥

The need to head over to a record store on a Wednesday, after work, didn't register as odd. In a funk, I assumed that was Romell's way of trying to cheer me up. He was *always* so flirty, how was I to distinguish this time from any other or take any of his gestures seriously. We'd been arguing, but I should've caught on in taxi ride back to his place. I should have figured as much, when I saw he started chewing all that gum so fast, seven pieces in about ten minutes. Silly me, I figured he was chewing all that gum and spitting it out just to annoy me, so I kept my back to him the entire ride and walked ahead of him into his building. We rode up to the thirty-seventh floor in separate elevators. As soon as he unlocked his door, I bolted into the living room. Even in my slim skirt and croc pumps, I was Flo Jo.

3

My leg banged into his marble cocktail table, sending it spinning around on its axis until the halves formed a circle. I dented my shin, but I wasn't rubbing my boo-boo. I jumped right on his Slinky sofa, leaned over it, reaching until I snatched my keys up off the rug. Then I made a beeline for the door, hoping I could run right out, but he blocked my exit. When I stepped to the left, he stepped to that side. When I tried to veer to the right, he kept right in front of me. I knew then he would not let me past. I had no choice but to get in his face, "What?"

"You don't wanna be with me?"

I shook my head.

"You don't wanna be with me?"

"No, I do not!"

"You show up in stilettos and a little skirt, and you expect me to believe you don't want me?"

"I did this for Spider."

"Well, Spider isn't here now. Is he? And, what about your poem?"

"What about it? I wanted you to know how I feel."

"Oh, so you admit you have feelings for me?"

"Pah–leese, Romell! That poem is about your situation."

"My situation, huh?"

"Yeah, that's the perfect solution."

"If you think you and I hookin' up would be the perfect solution, why don't you just say you want me?"

"Are you mental?"

"How long have you wanted me, Mia? How long?"

"Now, I know you've lost it. What makes you think I want you?"

"Your poem! I've got it right here." He patted himself down, pulled a page out of his back pocket and unfolded it in front of me. "There! You say all through this how you're gonna melt my fears away and how you're gonna make me feel."

I looked, reading aloud halfheartedly, "Chocolate Love every day can melt your fears away and have you feeling new. That's what Chocolate can do." Then, I shook my head. "And?"

He smacked his baldhead, paced and then, banged the back of it into the wall. "Chocolate, your last name is Love!"

"So? I wrote this to motivate you to embrace black love."

"Stop it. The only black Love you want me to embrace is you."

Now, I read the whole thing through. I could see how he could make that assumption. The words "Chocolate" and "Love" were both capitalized all the way through the poem, but I didn't do that intentionally. That connection didn't even occur to me when I jotted the lines down; my mind was in a totally different place. I laughed, but he didn't see humor in this, at all. His face was as stiff as steel.

I tried to explain. "I know how this looks, Romell, but that wasn't the meaning behind this. I meant chocolate as opposed to vanilla or any other flavor. Chocolate is a metaphor for black, and Love is just love, the emotion. Not my last name. That's just a coincidence."

"This ain't no coinki-dink! I told you once before. You won't be happy until I'm with a woman who's your height, your weight, and your complexion. What I should have said is you won't be happy, until I'm with you. Why won't you just admit it?"

"Hello! I am in a relationship with Spider. Remember him? Real tall, kinda goofy, I love him. Seriously, I was not coming on to you."

He stood, huffing and puffing for a moment, then looked at me hard. "Did you eat any peanuts?"

"No! What the hell kind of question is—"

I didn't finish my sentence. The next thing I knew, I felt his warm tongue, stroking mine and tickling the roof of my mouth. I heard the crackling of plastic when Romell's CD bags hit the carpet. Then, my bag dropped to the carpet, and I backed all the way to the wall, but the lower half of me began to wind as if it had a mind of its own. He grabbed my behind, pulled me into him, and boy oh boy. Now, when I walked in on Romell and Jun Ko, and saw him in those see-through drawers, I knew then: he wasn't packing peanuts there, either. Now that he was fully hard, I knew he could poke a hole in me if I let him, but still something inside me was aching for it.

I was so aroused, but it was as if the backs of my hands were glued to the wall. I couldn't bring myself to wrap my arms around him. To do so would've meant I was causing this to happen. As it stood, Romell initiated this. He was kissing me. Everything I was doing was involuntary. I wasn't stopping this, but I wasn't causing this, either. Technically, I wasn't responding. Kissing him back was only a reflex, a natural reaction to the stroke of his tongue, and the taste of spearmint, so he was kissing me. What I was feeling in my stomach I had no control over. This was my logic, and so by virtue of me keeping my hands to that wall and not "touching" him under any circumstances, I was not guilty.

Then, his hands started creeping their way up under my skirt. His lips left mine, traveled down my neck, and back up to my ear. "Chocolate, I need you," he whispered. I felt a jolt in my stomach—fear—next, my panties slipping off my behind. I opened one eye and saw Spider's face for a split second. That sent a chill through me, because in that instant, just like in our earlier staring match, Spider's hazel eyes bore into me. I shut mine tight now, but in my head, I could still hear his voice accusing, "If Romell is not in your bed, he's definitely on your mind."

Romell's face returned to mine. I felt his warm breath on my lips. He was panting, so was I. There was something in his eyes I'd never seen before. It scared me, because this part of me was supposed to belong to Spider. At Pookie's Jukebox, between those mirrors, it looked like there was two of me. Now, staring into Romell's eyes, I wished there were. He closed them and then moved in to kiss again, but I sealed my lips. Still he licked, enticing me to open. He felt so good and smelled so good, but I pressed my lips tighter. I had to. My conscience was taunting me.

Romell backed up. It looked as if his eyes were reading mine. He smirked. I watched his eyes grow wide, him moisten his lips and then, wink. Now, I was totally confused. I had no clue what to expect until I watched his head take a slow descent. I lost my breath and almost suffocated as Romell gave me a gentle nibble where Spider's mouth had never been. But, if this were to happen, there would be no way I could claim this was involuntary. No, if Romell went down on me, I had to be a willing participant; there was no disputing that. And quite honestly, I was more curious than anything else, especially since I always had this inkling that sexually, Romell would just blow me away. So, deep down inside, there was this secret place in me that always longed for this, even if it were only just once. This was not Spider, but I always wanted to experience a man's tongue there. But then again, this wasn't just any man. This was Romell. He was the one collecting my panties in his teeth. This was Romell dragging them down my thigh. I was already tingling. This was Romell, not Spider, and Romell had my panties at my ankles.

♥ ♥ ♥ ♥

I didn't ask for this. Spider was my man. He and I had been together since we were 15 years old. We'd just had a baby. Romell had been my closest friend since before I knew what my own name was. We were very close, inseparable even. And because Spider felt threatened by that, for whatever reason, he insisited that let him go. "I'm tired of this thing with you and Romell!"

Yeah, right! Romell was here before you! I didn't say that, instead I'd agreed. I wasn't supposed to be at Romell's now. But when I typed up that 'Chocolate Love' poem and pressed 'SEND' on the email that morning, I never expected anything like this.

My whole life, there had only been one kiss, one touch, one other body pressed to mine. There had only been one love. Well, maybe there wasn't just one *love*. Romell was in my past, in my dreams, and in my plans. So, Spider was right about that. Romell *was* on my mind. He was always in my thoughts, but he had never been in my bed, and that's why I slapped the shit out of him. Romell had my 99-cent-store panties down around my sister's shoes. I knew what was next, but I wasn't ready for it, and that's why I slapped the taste right out of his mouth. That noise cut through the air, bounced off the walls, and echoed. My hand hit the wall on the backswing, and now, my palm stung, and my fingers were throbbing. I shook my hand like it was rubber and then sucked my two middle fingers, two broken nails. I bit them off and spit them out. On my pinky, the chips in my polish had my airbrush looking like a Picasso, but that was the only thing I could think to do to prevent things from going any further.

Romell pressed his hand to his cheek and then examined his palm like he expected to see blood, all theatrics. Just like his staying on the floor was also theatrics. I didn't smack him to the ground. Romell was already down. He didn't expect to get slapped, so he lost his balance. He had no welts. He wasn't hurt. The only thing bruised was his ego. Now, he was trying to make me feel guilty. It wasn't working.

"Why didn't you just tell me to stop?" he asked.

I pulled my panties back up, instead of answering.

When he was all over me, I was fighting with myself. I was horny, so if I had managed to utter the word "stop" at that point, it would have sounded more like I was begging for it.

"I can't believe you did that," Romell said, and he stood back up.

"I can't believe what you were trying!" I tucked in my blouse.

He stood in my face. "I'm *trying* to show you how much I care!"

My half slip was gathered somewhere; I reached up and snatched it back down. "I'm getting married!"

He grabbed my left hand and held it up. "That man ain't marrying you!"

That had long been the consensus from Mommy and Dawn, but I didn't pay them any mind. Now that those words were coming from Romell, my armor was pierced, but I refused to let it show. "Don't say that!" I pulled away from him and stepped across the rug to put distance between us. Then I faced him. "Spider is gonna put a ring around my finger any day now!"

Romell stepped closer, folding his arms. He dropped his head, squinting at me. "And, what if he doesn't?"

"I'll put a ring around his eye! But no matter what, I will never sleep with you!"

"Never?"

"Never! You will *not* turn me into another Rubbermaid in your refrigerator, Romell Ulysses Goodwin!!"

"What the hell is that supposed to mean?"

"You had a quickie with Jun Ko last night, Romell, and today, here you are pulling down my panties?"

"You were enjoying it! So, why fight it? You want this." Romell said, and I couldn't help but look down. He stepped closer, repeating, "You want this." Those words grew softer each time.

I backed into the wall. My body still felt the impression of his hands. I don't know why, but I started to shake and couldn't stop, so fidgeting, I pretended the purse, plastic bags, and folded poem scattered on the carpet had my attention.

"Look at you. You can't hold still. You can't even look at me." He stepped all the way up and boxed me in with both arms, leaving me squirming. In his frigid apartment, all I felt was his body heat. I turned my head, keeping my lips together. He leaned in, stroking his nose against my cheek and neck for a moment, and then he growled in my ear, "You want me bad, and you don't even have a clue how good I can make *you* feel."

I snapped my head back so fast I almost got whiplash. I looked him dead in his eyes. "Yeah, me and everybody else."

He backed up. "What's that supposed to mean?"

I walked over, snatched up my carryall, turned, and gave him the most evil look I could muster.

Romell hung his head for a good minute. Then slowly, he collected the two white plastic bags off the floor. I watched him pull a CD out of each bag and tuck them under his arm. He came to me, stuffed the bags into my purse, and looked in my eyes. "Don't you see? I want you."

All my life I wanted to hear those words from him. He never settled for anything less than a "dime," so to me, this meant I was unofficially inducted into the "pretty girl" club; but now, somehow, I wasn't even flattered. I snapped at him, "Can't have everything you want."

"You know you want me, too!"

"Romell, if you're not satisfied with ten women, I ain't fool enough to think you'll be satisfied with me. You can have your dimes; you just can't have all the others and me. I'll be a dime. But I refuse to be your penny!" Now, I felt tears; wiping them with the heel of my hand, I watched Romell's posture go limp. I didn't want to cry here in front of him, so I slung the strap of my bag over my shoulder and walked toward the door.

"Mia, wait," and it was strange; he sounded sad. I stopped in my tracks. "Stay, please? We don't have to do anything; we don't even need to be in the same room. I just really need your company right now."

His coaxing gave me more chills. He seemed sincere, but I still didn't turn around. I shook my head and continued to walk.

"Mia, please! Don't go. Stay even if it's just for a little while." He rarely begged. I turned my head slightly, not wanting to look directly at him. Out of the corner of my eye, I could see him against the wall, head resting in the crook of one arm, while the other dangled. Something was bothering him. I could sense it. I wasn't sure if it was what had just happened or if it was something else, but *something* was wrong. I looked at the door only a couple steps away. That latch was calling me, sounding raspy just like Spider. I wasn't even supposed to be here. But, Romell needed me. Those few times he was vulnerable, I did everything in my power to make him feel better. I could do that then, because sex was never a threat. There was this invisible barrier between us: a line neither of us dared to cross. Frankly, I didn't know if I could comfort him now without crossing that line.

"Come on, Chocolate. Please."

His voice, now distraught, went straight through me. I dropped my head and sighed, ready to turn around. Then, reaching out for my hand, he said, "I promise I won't try anything." I knew him so well; *that* was enough to make me pick my head up, take steady steps, and close the door...on my way out.

Do We Have Tomorrow?

T RAFFIC WAS LIGHT HEADING UP THE F.D.R. Drive. The air that blustered into the backseat blew my curls every which way, but I had no choice but to keep the windows open, sorry to be in the only yellow taxi with no AC. My sweaty body was sticking to the vinyl, but my mind, elsewhere, was way too distracted to focus; the map of Manhattan inches in front of me was actually a blur. A few times, I even caught myself unconsciously peeling back the edges. Sticker glue now coated the only halfway decent nail left on that hand. Out the window, a barge was coming down, now under the 59th Street Bridge. Moving slowly, it was barely breaking waves in the grey water. I could clearly see that because both the bridge and the barge were as big as day, but my mind was still where I left my fingernails, back at Romell's.

I promise I won't try anything. That would've worked for Spider, but then again, had Spider said that, it would not have been just another line. Spider never played games like that. If he said something, he meant it. He almost never made promises. He never had to. His word was good enough, especially since I had yet to catch him in a lie.

Romell, on the other hand, always kept a hidden agenda. Of all the men I'd ever known, he was the smoothest, but Romell wasn't always the smooth talker. Once upon a time, he was almost always at a loss for words. I had a smart mouth, so in high

13

school, when he approached me with his 50 spiral-notebook-jagged-edged pages stapled together. A handwritten script full of pickup and rejection lines, it was the most pathetic thing *I* ever saw, but I understood Romell. Everything was a science to him, a formula that had to be figured out.

A little while? I know him. If things had gone Romell's way, Spider would not have seen me until morning. We would have sat on that rug, talked, drunk something potent. Then, he would've claimed he needed a shower. *I promise I won't try anything,* top of page 27. *Nothing will happen that you don't want to happen,* bottom of page 27. Bottom of page 50, *I never said I was your man.* I shook my head, thinking. *That hard-on must've drawn blood from your brain. Hello! If you teach me your tricks, don't use those same tricks on me and expect them to work. Am I right or wrong? Outdated mating tactics. Typical. Who was he fooling with that?* Good thing I came to my senses. I was surprised he didn't follow me to the elevator, but I knew why he didn't. That ego took a beating. *Oh, well.* I knew he'd get over it sooner or later. Just like I knew if I didn't make it home before Spider, I'd have some serious explaining to do.

♥ ♥ ♥ ♥

I made it back to my building with light still in the sky. I love summer. A bright sky gave me a good enough excuse; I simply lost track of time. Ringing for the elevator, I looked over my shoulder to the stairwell. There, an orange Converse peeked out from around the corner. I walked over and sat down on the cracked step. Dressed in his Chicken Shack orange, Jeff was slumped forward, resting his head on his arms. His nest of light brown curls spilled over his knees, exposing the back half of his hair, which was faded to a hairline, squared across his pale, freckled neck. I nudged him awake.

He straightened out his body and yawned. "Damn,

gurl. What hours do *you* work?"

I didn't answer that. "What brings you here?"

"I came to apologize," Jeff said smiling.

"I'm glad you decided to work things out with Spider," I said.

"Fuck him! It's *you* I wanna say sorry to." Jeff looked at me. My confusion must've registered on my face, because he continued. "Look, I realize all the times I was taking advantage, I was using *you,* and that ain't right. And, about what happened at Lola's, I'm sorry I shook you up like that."

"You didn't shake me up."

"Mia, your ass was shook."

"I wasn't afraid of you. I was afraid for Tee-Bo's safety. You broke all that damn glass when I had my baby in the room. So, if you're going to apologize, don't apologize because you think you scared me. Apologize because you put my child in danger."

"I hear you, and like I said, I really *am* sorry."

"Okay, Jeff. Just don't let it happen again. I know you're not coming up, so I guess I'll see you later," I said reaching to pull myself up.

"Wait!" Jeff said. "There's something else I wanna talk to you about."

"What is it?"

"Your sister."

"What about Dawn?"

"Yo, Mia. Ever since I met her at the hospital when Tee-Bo was born, I can't stop thinking about her. I had a long talk with her in the waiting room. She's got a good head on her shoulders, and her personality is just as beautiful as her face."

"Dawn's got two faces."

"Don't bad mouth your sister."

"Apologize to your brother."

Jeff rolled his eyes and spat through the banister into the stairwell. "Mia, I ain't dealing with none of them no more. I'm done! This thing with Pop's ashes is where I draw the line. Bad enough they did what

15

they did to Lola."

"Who's they?"

"This crazy woman, Barbara, and Pop's wife, Mae Mae."

"Dr. Snyder? What did Dr. Snyder do?"

"She set Lola up, and Barbara tried to kill Lola."

"How did Dr. Snyder set Lola up?"

"She told Barbara that Lola slept with that crazy woman's husband."

"Well, did she?"

"Did she what?"

"Did Lola sleep with the woman's husband?"

"Don't matter! They were all supposed to be friends!"

"Friends?" Now it all made sense. That's why the woman in the melted picture at Dr. Snyder's looked so familiar. That was Lola when she was much younger.

"Yeah. And they cut my mother up bad. She's still suffering. She didn't deserve *that*."

I didn't know what to say. That was Lola in Dr. Snyder's wedding picture. Now, the whole situation made perfect sense. Dr. Snyder did say her friends call her Mae Mae, and Lola *did* call her Mae Mae. If Lola, Barbara, and Dr. Snyder were all supposed to be friends, and Lola was sleeping with both of their husbands, I can see why they flipped the way they did. Now, I understood why Dr. Snyder was so bitter. Maybe it was part guilt, but I still felt she needed to get over it; that was decades ago. I shook my head. There was more to this situation than I had realized. No one person gave me the whole truth. It had to be pieced together like my quilt, but I was willing to bet any amount of money that Barbara was Dr. Snyder's friend Babs. This situation went deep. Jackie may have pissed me off, but she was right about one thing: this wasn't any of my business. On that note, I decided to stay out of it. I looked at Jeff's sad, green eyes and shrugged. "I understand how you feel, and

I'm sorry all that had to happen. But, you've got to realize they *all* made mistakes back then. So, it's best to just let the past be the past."

He shook his head. "It ain't that easy, Mia. I still don't know where Pop's ashes are."

"I understand, Jeff, but what can you do?"

"I don't know. I think I'll need me a blunt to answer that one." He looked at me and half smiled, then added, "But, Lola said I should just pray on it."

I stood and dusted off my skirt. "That sounds like a plan. Thanks for the apology, Jeff. Now, I really do need to get going."

"Wait, Mia! What about your sister?"

I shook my head. "Jeff, don't even waste your breath. My sister is a gold digger with a big ol' shovel."

"Maybe so, but not everyone would sign up to be your Lamaze coach." Jeff said. To be honest, Spider wanted to, but I was too afraid he couldn't handle it. After the stunt with the sonogram, I wasn't letting him anywhere near the delivery room. I looked back at Jeff. He pushed his long hair out of his eyes. They grew big, and their sparkle returned. "Dawn," Jeff paused, smiling. "She was there the whole time making sure you had everything you needed, and she kept those doctors and nurses on their toes. I see *that* as a beautiful thing."

I sighed. I knew Jeff was right about that, but I still preferred to be angry with her so I said, "When are you gonna cut that hair, Jeff?"

He twisted his lips. "You keep changing the subject on me! And what do you mean get it cut? I just got my hair cut."

"No, I mean a *real* haircut. You shouldn't be working around food with all that mess on your head. When are you gonna shave it off?"

"Never, I got all the hairnets I need."

"I still think that's unsanitary. I'm sure they're stressing you about your hair at work."

"Yeah," he sighed. "I think I'm gonna braid it. You know where I can get that done?"

"None of your baby mamas braid?" I snapped, watching him run his fingers through that mess of curls. He smiled again and shook his head. I smiled back. "I know a beauty salon."

"I ain't going up in a beauty salon to get my hair braided with a bunch of girlies."

"Trust me, Jeff. You're gonna *love* this salon. There's no place else like it."

He cut his eye at me in disbelief. "Can I get cornrows?"

"You can get crop circles if that's what you want."

He clapped his hands. "Aa–ight! What's this place called?"

I said, "Head to Toe." I didn't know if that was totally evil or the sweetest thing I'd ever done, but I could pretty much guess Dawn would cuss me out and Jeff would thank the hell outta me. I laughed, but even if Dawn did cuss me out, it would be worth it.

Should I Celebrate?

BACK IN MY EMPTY APARTMENT, I SAT MY BAG down at the foot of the bed, dove onto the mattress, gathered an armful of pillows, and snuggled my chin into the pile. Alone and in silence, this was a good time to reflect. For a very long time, I felt things would work out just fine between Spider and me. Now, I wasn't so sure. I didn't know whether to fight or give up. I didn't know how Spider and I would work everything out; I just knew we had to. He was my whole world. Part of me felt like I was fighting a lost cause, but I had to fight, had to keep pushing, because that's what I lived for. If I didn't, there was nothing left for me to do but die. Fight or give up? Fight. I had no choice: my life depended on it.

With that on my mind, I pulled out my poetry journal, and wiped the tear from my eyelash. I cut my light on, crawled back into bed, and stared at the blank page; it was wide-ruled. I usually tried to camouflage my emotions with metaphors when I wrote in my journal. However, under the circumstances and as hopeless as I felt, hopelessness was what I wrote, even though my feelings were purged in poetic form.

We had yesterday.
Do we have tomorrow?

19

Should I celebrate?
Or drown my sorrows?
I wanna fight
When there's no wins,
Still I want you with me.

I'm hanging on
For dear life.
Nothing's working,
Now, I don't know what else to try.
We go through the motions
And pretend.
Is this the beginning of the end?

You're doing your thang.
I'm doing mine.
I wanna feel needed
And loved
Like the good ol' times,
But you ignore me.
That's how it's been.
Is this the beginning of the end?

Cold winter days,
Hot summer nights,
I felt so complete
In your arms,
As you held me tight.
Will you ever hold me
That way again?
Is this the beginning of the end?

I'd be okay
With what we had.
I realize our worst
Was not that bad.
Now, you have your goals.
I have my plans.
And, we're not connecting.

At least before
You and I,
We were talking
And not reading each other's minds.
Did you give up
When I gave in?
Is this the beginning of the end?

4 some reason,
4 some cause,
4 some strange reason,
It's just not obvious.

Please show me
What I don't see
What's the reason?
4 the problem

I closed my journal and slid it back between the mattresses. Then, I took a deep breath and sobbed. I hadn't felt this way in a long time. The last time I felt like giving up, I gave in. As a result, Tee-Bo was born. What was I going to do now? I didn't want to raise my son in a household with any other man, so I had to keep at it. Somehow, I had to draw strength from somewhere and keep on fighting for this relationship. *Spider didn't say I looked good. That's okay. Back in high school, he called me "Pretty Mia." I'll hold on to that. He doesn't tell me he loves me. That's okay, too. Back in high school, he told me he wanted love. Back then, he made me feel so special because he noticed me. I'll hold on to those memories and give this relationship all I have, once and for all.*

We were too close to getting married to stop now. Spider said we had issues. Now, I had to face them. One was money. That wasn't an issue now because of that big check he just received, and the record label just gave him a promotion, so I knew he finally would have a salary coming. Another issue was trust. He

21

said I didn't trust him. That was hard. We just agreed to cut everybody else off, so I didn't have to worry about that issue, either. Then, there was loyalty. He felt I put everyone else ahead of him. That was funny; I had always gone out of my way to accomodate his family because I thought winning their approval would, in turn, satisfy him. But somehow, in the process, I managed to piss off everyone: his family and mine. Now, I didn't think there was anyone else I could even try to put ahead of Spider, except Tee-Bo. As for Romell, he had always been my very best friend. Now, we couldn't go back to being just friends. The curiosity alone would kill me. I had no choice but to leave him alone and make sure Spider never found out what almost happened. My silver link bracelet dangled from my wrist. It was funny how, after all the times Romell asked me to wear it, the one time I wore it when we were together, he didn't even notice. That was just as well. The bracelet was a beautiful thought, but now I needed to let that go and focus on Spider and Spider only. I unfastened it and slid it back between the mattresses. So now none of our issues were issues at all. I just needed to convince Spider that we made progress so that we could hurry up and get married.

Spider didn't like me touching his old, suitcase record player, but I reached over and turned the radio on. Of course, every third station was playing "Be Happy." As much as I loved Mary J., I didn't appreciate her now. How could I ever hear that again and not think of Romell? I needed to hear a song that reminded me of Spider. I changed the dial and heard James Ingram and Patti Austin, "How Do You Keep the Music Playing?" That was it. I left the station right there, lying on my bed, listening to the radio, until eventually, they played an old song by the Jones Girls, "You're Gonna Make Me Love Somebody Else."

I was singing or, better yet, screaming at the top of my lungs. I didn't hear Spider unlock the door or enter the apartment, but he walked into the bedroom with his dress shirt half buttoned revealing the scooped neck of his undershirt, his red tie in his hand. He cut his eye at me with a snide comment, "Who's the somebody else, your boyfriend downtown?"

This was exactly what I was trying to avoid. I massaged my temples, saying, "You're giving me a headache."

"Good. Now we're even. Sometimes being with you feels like a game of musical chairs," he said. "I don't wanna be left standing alone when the music stops."

I cut the music off. "Since you don't want to be left *standing* alone, when do you think we'll be *standing* at the altar?"

"I don't know about that. We have a lot of issues to work out. There are a lot of changes that need to be   made."

"There you go again with these so-called issues. Why do you keep saying that?"

"Because, with you it's all or nothing. That's an issue."

Another issue? "I am not that bad. How is it all or nothing?"

He looked at me like I was crazy. Then he shook his head. "Why do you have such a problem with me having friends who are female?"

"Spider, once you start off sharing secrets, you end up sharing everything else."

"Is that what happened with you and Romell?" Now, he stared at me.

I was thinking. *Oh, damn. What does he know?* And even though his hazel eyes felt like they were probing my conscience, I still managed to utter a cool, "Absolutely not."

"Then, what makes you so sure that'll happen with me? For all I know, you could've been with him tonight, but I trust you. I always have. So, it's about time you started trusting me."

Not the trust thing again. "Okay, Spider. I'll try, but it's hard. Especially since I know you were just with Pilar doing who knows what?"

"Mia, that was another all-nighter at the label; Pilar was just there taking the minutes."

"Why? Because you feel I didn't make time for you? Spider, you lied to me!"

"I didn't lie to you."

"You were supposed to go to your mother's. Instead you spent the night with some other girl? You lying, no good, cheating, low down, dirty, no count, trifling—"

"Mia, stop! Stop jumping to conclusions, and listen to me for once. You never listen to me, and that's another issue!"

"If it ain't one thing it's another! Okay! Okay, Spider. I'm all ears *now*. What do you have to say for yourself?"

"I didn't leave here to be with anybody else. I went to my mother's, but I couldn't get in. She changed the locks."

"She did?" Having those keys meant a lot to me. I sighed then looked up at Spider. "Is that why you called your mother and cursed her out?"

"Who told you?"

"Jackie called this morning," I said. Spider looked away as I continued, "I can understand you being upset because your mother changed the locks. But why did you have to go to that girl's house?"

"I didn't go to her house! I went back to the label. They were having an all-night brainstorming session. Pilar is the secretary, and she was there taking the minutes."

"The minutes?"

"Notes from the meeting. Afterwards, Pilar took the time to type my résumé for me."

I sucked my teeth. "It still seems like she was taking *my* time," I mumbled.

"That's because you assume the worst and don't

pay attention to what I say."

"If I don't pay attention, it's because you don't say what I need to hear anymore. Back in high school...you called me Pretty Mia."

"I never said that."

"Yes, you did. You called me Pretty Mia the day you asked me to be your tutor."

"I would never have called you Pretty Mia."

I gasped, "Why the hell not?"

"Pretty Mia was the tall girl who wore that stink perfume and way too much makeup."

"If she wore too much makeup, why did you call *her* pretty?"

"Because she was always made up, even for gym class."

I shook my head. "Well, if I wasn't Pretty Mia, then who was I?"

"I would've called you Short Mia."

"I am not short!"

"I'm six-foot-five! You're short *to me!*"

"Okay fine, Spider, but that day, you *did* say you wanted love!"

"I didn't say that! I was fourteen years old!"

"Yes, you did! You told me if I was Mia Love you wanted me to be your tutor, and I asked you why. Now, I remember this like it was yesterday; your exact words were, 'Because, I want me a love'!"

"Huh-ha, huh-ha, huh-ha, huh-ha, huh-ha!" Spider was laughing so hard, tears were coming out of his eyes.

"What's so funny!"

"Mia Love is your name, stupid!"

When he said that, it hit me. *He meant "Mia Love," not "me a love." He was saying my name; he wasn't expressing an interest in me. He wasn't looking for love at all. All he had wanted was a tutor: He wanted me, Mia Love, to be his tutor, and that was all he wanted—a tutor.* I buried my face in my hands to try to stop myself from crying, but my nose was running.

My face was all snot and tears. Had I known what he really meant back then, I would have acted accordingly. I wouldn't have spent so much time with him. Or made the first move to kiss him. And I definitely wouldn't have set my sights on him when my heart was set on Romell. Now, it made sense, why Spider never planned to marry me, and why he never told me he loved me. This relationship happened by accident. Not because he wanted me. A misunderstanding sparked the chain of events that led us to where we were at this point in our lives. So, what was reality now? If Spider never said that, who was he, and who was I?

All I'd ever done was try to be what Spider and everybody else thought I should be, but who was I really? Before Spider and I got together, my high school was my high school. After we got together, his college became my college, his major became my major, his life became my life, and his beliefs became my beliefs. My only goal was to love him the best that I could. I prided myself by believing a woman's love didn't get any better than mine. My only plan was for Spider and me to get married and buy a house. For that reason, I went out of my way to win his family over. To me, Spider became everything, my reason for existence, my life, and my future; he became the one I lived for. If what I based our relationship on didn't happen, what did we have? What was my purpose? Where was my life going? What would I cling to now?

Before, when he told me he never wanted to get married, my hopes were shattered. That was nothing compared to this. My entire life was all for nothing, especially since Spider found it so necessary to clarify; he gave no forethought to how this revelation would affect me. At the very least, he should've cared enough to spare my feelings.

Still with his tie in his hand, Spider leaned down and wrapped his arm around me. Now, after he'd just ripped my heart out and stomped on it, he felt the need to console a sistah. I could feel the knot of his tie in my back, "Mia, that don't matter. You know how I feel now."

I shook him off. "I know how you feel? How am I supposed to know you love me if you never say it?"

"Love is not what I say. Love is what I do."

"Love is what you do?"

"Yes. Every day I come home to you. I ignore all the flirting women out in the street, and *I* come home."

"You ain't doing me any favors, Negro! You come home to free room, board, housekeeping, laundry service, child care, and automatic bill pay. That's not love! That's convenience!"

"How could you say that? All right then, since this is about money, let me know what I owe you, and I'll pay you back."

"Fuck your money! If you really loved me, you would have married me a long time ago! Instead, you dangle that promise and use our issues as an excuse to try to change me!"

"Changes need to be made!"

"If you feel so many changes need to be made, start with your damn self!"

"Mia, we *do* have issues."

"So what! I'm tired of holding on and waiting for you to be totally satisfied. That'll never happen, so I'm not wasting any more time, Spider!"

"What?"

"I said I am not wasting any more time with you."

His brows squeezed together like an accordion. "You're not gonna waste any more time with me?"

"That's what I said!" I stomped over to the bedroom door and yanked it open. My hand went on my hip, and I pointed out. "Spider, you gots–ta go!"

He plopped on the bed. His tie fell to the floor, and he dropped his head in his palms.

So I screamed, "You heard me! Git!"

After a while, he rose from the bed and parted his

lips, but there was a long pause before the words came out. "If that's the way you feel, then I don't wanna be here," he said, like he had a choice. He unclipped his keys from his slacks and tossed them on the bed. "I left the other set at work, but don't worry. I'll give them back to you." He looked around the room one final time. Then, he hung his head and sulked toward the door.

"Spider, wait!" I said. He stopped and faced me. I looked into his hazel eyes and watched the light wane as I said, "Don't forget to take that cat with you."

Or Drown My Sorrows?

*T*HAT WAS THAT. I HEARD SPIDER'S FEET DRAG down the hall and Joy scamper inside the pet carrier. The front door squeaked open and then slammed shut. That's when I left the bedroom and made my way to the door. I peeked through the peephole. I didn't see Spider on the other side; he was gone. I put him out, and he was gone. Now, I started talking to myself. "I already know what Dawn's going to say about this but I did not just put Spider's ass out, because I'm stressed. I am not stressed! I put him out because I'm fed up. There's a difference. Stressed means I'm losing it. I'm not losing it; I'm just sick of him. I'm fed up; that's all. I'm fed up!" I locked all four locks, took a deep breath, and then threw my fist in the air. "Yes! That was invigorating! I should have a party."

I leaped onto the loveseat and smiled, staring into the ceiling's white stucco. It reminded me of Spider, nice to look at, but served no other purpose whatsoever. He wasn't a bad person; he was just hard to tolerate. One, he was withdrawn. I was always one to speak my mind. I needed communication. Not just complaints, I needed conversation. Talk to me about *my* interests. Ask me how *I'm* feeling. Ask me how *my* day was once in a while. He never did that. Two, he was insensitive. He didn't appreciate a thing I did. That made me feel my efforts were a waste. I was starved for a compliment, which led me to number three. As fine as he was, his greatest flaw was his lack of charm. He never flirted. He had the prettiest lips I'd ever seen on a man, but he never licked them, unless he was out of Chapstick. Those lips never whispered in my ear, sending chills through me the way Romell's did. And as dreamy as Spider's eyes were, he never winked; he just didn't do things like that. He didn't flirt. He didn't tease. His timing was always off. His idea of getting dressed was to throw on his jersey, khakis, and Hush Puppies. He had no style, no sense of humor, and no zest for life. He was just...there. A gorgeous face, a six-foot-five-inch body, ripped with muscle, but not the least bit interested in sex on any day other than Saturday. And, that was Spider. What a waste!

Sadly, I was always aware of how Spider was. It was obvious that he was nonchalant the first time I saw him shrug his shoulders. It was reconfirmed every time I heard him say, "Fine, whatever." I just didn't know what to make of it; I couldn't tell if it was submission or disinterest. I recognized it as apathy around the same time I had also realized there was this wall guarding his emotions. But, by then, I was already in love with him; so of course, I made it my mission to be the one who would personally help him heal. But hey, I loved Spider. He had an innocence I had never seen in a guy; that was one of the reasons why I fell for him. I loved him, even though he was withdrawn, insensitive, and well...strange. He still had all his old toys. His Star Trek space ship, Evil Knievel, and Stretch Armstrong he kept in the original boxes. He wasn't particularly interested in cars. Only Spider could go to work, drive a Ferrari, a Bentley, and a Rolls, and still consider that a terrible day. He had strange ways and did all kinds of strange things, but I loved him. Because of that, if he couldn't marry me, at the very least, he should've appreciated me. I never got what I needed from him. After all these years, I had enough of that, but that was more than ten years wasted, and now, I had his baby to raise. So, I wondered. *What am I going to do now?*

All I knew was Spider. He was predictable. I knew his patterns. I knew his routines. I understood why he thought what he thought and did what he did. He rarely surprised me. I was only disappointed when I tried to turn him into what I wanted him to be. But I knew what he was. I had always known what he was; since I first met him in high school, he'd barely changed. We were together for over ten years, lived together, had a baby together, and even had a joint bank account: all this to break up. *This* was not supposed to happen. *We* were supposed to get married. No ifs, ands, or buts about it. Now, here I was twenty-six years old with no husband, no man, no money, no plan, a dead-end job, no degree, and a newborn baby. I couldn't help but think about that, at times out loud.

After all these years with Spider, I am not supposed to hunt for a new man. After ten years of ColecoVision, being his typist, and hiding his Hush Puppies, how am I supposed to move on to someone else? This is silly. I'm not going to even worry about that. I'll just do what everybody else does. I'll go out. If I meet someone that seems nice, I'll give him my phone number. Then, if I get to know him well enough and I find him attractive, eventually, I'll have sex with him. Just that thought gave me the heebee geebees; my skin started to crawl. *How am I going to sleep with a total stranger? I couldn't even get myself to sleep with Romell, and I've known him all my life. I couldn't sleep with Romell, and I've had a crush on him forever. And to top it all off, he's the sexiest man I've ever known. Still, I could not bring myself to give him some booty, Romell, of all people—sexy ass, lip-licking, panty-biting Romell. So how on earth was I supposed to climb into bed with some less than perfect stranger who, for all I know, could have a rusty butt and stinky feet? I can't. Romell is as sexy as they come. If I can't sleep with him, I can't sleep with anybody. I can't date. I've never been on a date before in my entire life. I've always been with Spider. So what the hell am I supposed to do now?*

Even if I could get myself to date, who would want me? I'm no striking beauty like my sister. And, unlike Jun Ko, I don't own a beauty spa and have a master's degree from Columbia. I am as regular as they come. I'm a collection agent, the only one at the agency who's been there for more than two years and has yet to advance to the legal department. Tears spilled down. *My ass is on written warning for taking so many days off to help folks out.* I chuckled and wiped my face. *I'm one step away from disciplinary and two steps away from suspension. There's nothing fabulous about me. I don't belly dance; I don't hang-glide; I don't have my pilot's license. So, who's going to want me? And what man in this day and age wants a ready-made family? Raising another man's child was popular back in the eighties. That was then, this is now. The days of the stepdad putting another man's child through college went out of style with the black leather blazers, tams, and skinny ties. So, I will never find a man, and I will never get married. I will be single until the day I die lonely, bitter, and depressed.* I punched my throw pillow and threw it across the room. That didn't help. I wished I were dead.

My eyes were teary, looking from the stucco down across my painted walls. *This blue is such a dreary color. This wall was supposed to be pink—cotton candy pink to be exact. There's no life to this color; it's a flat, ugly blue. I hate it. I wanted the color scheme for this room to be brown, cream, beige and cotton candy pink. I only painted it periwinkle because Spider thought the pink was too feminine. But the pink would have been the right color to soften up the browns from the leather chair and the chests, and that would have given this whole room just the right balance. I knew what the hell I was talking about. I* had everything mapped out—soft color on the wall, accents throughout the room in a slightly darker shade of pink for coherence.

"Periwinkle is damn near hospital blue; it's ugly." *I'll have to repaint. Then, if I do paint the walls over, I'll have to change the throw pillows. The flowers on the chaise are blue; I'll have to change that. And the crystal. I don't know when I'll be able to do all that. I work at the only company in America where the raises don't keep up with the rise in the cost of living. That's messed up, because Spider doesn't have a thing to worry about. He just came into money, and he just got a promotion. He's set. He can do whatever he wants. Me, I will always be short of either money or time, working two and three jobs to make ends meet, trying to be both mother and father to my son. Mommy did what she had to do. She worked it out, but I am raising a boy, that's not as easy. I will be struggling, but not Spider. Oh, no. Spider is going to go out and find somebody else, probably Asia or what's-her-name, Pilar. Who knows? He may even be with one of them right now. Whoever it is, he may not marry the bitch, but I'll bet he'll move her to a nice big house in the suburbs.*

That's okay though. My bills are paid. And if I ever need extra money, I could collect bottles. I sighed. *Going to the supermarket with a billfold full of coupons is bad enough; I don't want to be seen with black garbage bags full of dirty bottles. Then again, I could always wash them. No, the bottle thing is almost as bad as going down to the Willis Avenue Bridge with Windex and a squeegee. I could borrow a few dollars from Dawn, and I could always ask Romell for money. On second thought, I'd rather collect bottles.* I took a deep breath and slowly exhaled. *What am I worrying for? It's not like I'm in danger of getting evicted. Jeff got evicted and had to move in with Lola. Things are not that bad for me. But, if things got tough, I could always move in with Mommy.* I rolled my eyes. *I'd rather rent a room in Spider's basement. His house will be big enough; I'm sure. Forget that. I'd sell my tail. I wonder how the girls on Hunts Point are dressing. This is crazy; I am not going to sell my ass. Not like that's an option, anyway. I couldn't give it away with a coupon.* I closed my eyes tight and shook my head. "Stop it. Stop it! Everything is going to be fine."

Of course things are going to be fine...for Spider. He will be just fine in his house. I bet his house will have four or five bedrooms. A deck. A front lawn. A nice big pool in the back. A Jacuzzi. Yep, Spider will be just fine in that great big house of his. Poked out, my lips began to cramp from tension. I stretched them, moving them all around. Then, I sniffled. *That was supposed to be my house. Now, I'll never have a house. And, I'll never have a husband. That man took the best years of my life. I'll be stuck here, in this dump with my junkyard crap forever.* "Oh! I really wish I were dead." *It's not like I have anything to look forward to. I might as well get it over with right now.* "That's exactly what I'm going to do."

I Wanna Fight...

OW CAN I KILL MYSELF? THE ONLY QUICK AND *painless way I know of is a gunshot to the head, but I don't know anybody who has a gun except Uncle Buster from Columbia, SC who's always shooting trespassers, so a gunshot is out. What are my other options? I could jump off a building, slit my wrist, or overdose on pills.*

I am not jumping off the roof of this building. My building is only seven stories high. If I mess around and survive the fall, my ass will end up in a wheelchair. Then what? No, I am not jumping off this building. "Okay, then, I'll slit my wrist." I jumped up and went to the kitchen. I snatched open my utensil drawer, and pulled out the spatula, ladle, ice cream scooper, the nutcracker, bottle opener, meat tenderizer, the potato peeler, and my serving spoons. Now, all that was left in my drawer was the cutlery. I picked up my decorating knife and examined the rippled blade. I dropped it back in the drawer. *I ain't making no damn crinkle-cut French fries.* I grabbed my paring knife. Its blade had a straight edge, but it wasn't very sharp, so I chucked it back into the drawer. The sharpest knives I had were the tomato knife, the bread knife, and any one of my steak knives. My tomato knife would slice tomatoes paper-thin. My bread knife was so sharp; the first time I used it, I had given myself a nasty cut across the palm of my hand as I sliced a bagel. That taught me to stand the bagel on its end and slice downward away from my hand. So, I knew that knife was sharp. And as for my steak knives, even when I didn't tenderize, they sliced through meat like butter. I looked at the serrated edges of the bread and tomato knives. Then, I looked closely at the ridges and sharp stainless steel teeth of one of my steak knives and realized how drastic this was. "I ain't cuttin' myself for nobody!" I hurled the knives back into the drawer and slammed it shut.

All right, so what's in the medicine cabinet? I hurried to the bathroom and snatched it open. All I had was Motrin and Tums. "This won't kill me. And, if I mess around and try to overdose, I'll have to get my stomach pumped. That'll hurt." I closed my cabinet. *Okay, so I'm not going to kill myself, even though I know I told Mommy I couldn't live without Spider. I hung on for so long, because I felt without him I'd have nothing else to live for. Spider is fine, but not fine enough to cause myself any physical pain.*

I stormed into the bedroom. Seeing Spider's cluster of cologne bottles on the dresser, I knocked them across the room. Tears made their way down my cheeks again. *That ain't hurting Spider; I bought those.* I looked at his suitcase record player in the corner. The first time he saw me get too close to it, he had a titty attack. He snapped at me, "Don't touch that!" Well now, I marched myself over to his side of the room and knocked his little record player right to the floor. It came down with a crash and the top popped off. I sucked in a deep breath and blew hard. Now, I felt somewhat better. But still, I climbed onto my bed and cried some more.

Why am I so upset? It wasn't like I was happy with him. He didn't appreciate me. He was a jerk. We didn't kick back and enjoy each other's company; he frustrated the hell out of me. I didn't look forward to the time I spent with him. I enjoy my time with Romell. Romell's easy to talk to. I can talk to him about anything. I've always gotten along with him. He appreciates me; he tries to take care of me to the point where it almost sickens me sometimes. I took another breath. *And as far as charm goes, Romell oozes it. I thought I couldn't live without Spider. It's okay, though; I still have Romell.*

I laughed. *If Romell knew how I felt right now, I'm sure he would say something to make me laugh. Then, he'd find some subtle way of telling me how wrong I am. He lets me vent, and unlike Dawn, I don't have to worry about him repeating anything I say. He's my best friend in the whole wide world. And, Romell is the only one who calls me Chocolate. Chocolate Love.* I smiled. *Maybe, that's not such a bad idea. I did have that dream about him when I was twelve and all the other ones after that. Actually feeling his lips on mine was way sweeter than anything I'd ever dreamed. That kiss was a sugar rush. We were so close to doing it, too; he had my panties in his teeth. And Romell is so...sexy—his voice, his walk, his eyes, his skin; the way he smiles, winks, and moistens those lips. Sexy?* I laughed again. *He's scrumptious.* I now wiped tears from my face. *Crying...in bed—this is not the way I am going to spend the rest of my evening. If I must cry, I might as well put my tears to good use. If I spend tonight in bed, better Romell's than mine. And, I know his sexy ass is going to be all over me.*

I picked up the phone and dialed his number. As soon as Romell answered, I said, "It's over."

"What's over?"

"Spider and I broke up. He just left."

"He'll be back tomorrow."

"No, he's not coming back!"

"Trust me, Chocolate. He'll show up in the morning."

"What makes you so sure?"

"Only a fool would let a good thing slip away, and Spider Snyder's no fool."

"That's what you think! It's over! And, I don't want him back! Ever!"

Romell yawned, then said, "You say that now, but you two are gonna work it out." Not getting the reaction I'd anticipated, I opened up and let loose a wave of tears. Once my sniffles slowed to a steady rhythm of gentle sighs, Romell sighed, too and said, "Don't cry, Chocolate."

"Don't tell me not to cry! If anything, offer me your shoulder."

He paused, but then he said, "All right. If my shoulder is what you need, you're welcome to it."

"Okay," I quickly agreed. "I'll be right down." After I hung up, I took the fastest bath in history. I jumped in and out of the tub sloshing apricot-scented, oily water onto the bathroom floor then took slippery steps back to the bedroom. In a frenzy, I yanked my dresser drawers open and sifted through heaps of bras and panties. Thanks to Mommy's priceless advice on feminine hygiene, all my panties were cotton. The only decent bras I owned were nursing bras—ugly, white, orthopedic-looking nursing bras. None of this would be as enticing as a red, lace thong. Even Dr. Snyder had a sexy nightie. I owned nothing that was lacy, silky, satin, or see-through. *I could've sworn I had a plain black bra somewhere.* Rummaging through the odd assortment of scarves, wraps, and belts in my bottom drawer, I stumbled across my hot pink bikini bathing suit. I stretched the bikini top over my exploding breasts. Having missed so many feedings, they were sore and by now probably two cup sizes larger. The teeny, tiny, bikini top didn't look like it had enough fabric to cover the girls, but it was better than nothing. I slid into it. Then, I pulled out my one pair of Daisy Dukes and held them up. When Dawn insisted on buying these shorts for me, I looked at her like she was crazy. I swore I would never wear them. Now, I snatched off the tag. It was funny how never could happen so soon.

I tipped into Romell's, wearing a fresh coat of

makeup among other things. His gaze traveled down my white tank top with my pink bikini strap peeking out, down my well-oiled, exposed legs all the way to the pointy tips of my pumps. He cocked his head and squinted. "Why are you wearing heels at this time of night?" he asked.

My voice steeped with innocence. "They match my bag."

I expected him to walk behind me so that he could check me out; he didn't. He shrugged instead and stepped quickly into the living room. He sat down on his sectional. I strolled over, and sat beside him. Leaning closer, I tried to cross my legs. The stiff denim of my shorts was gathering into my feminine parts and cutting off the circulation in my thighs as I tried to swing my leg over. I gave up that thought, returning my foot to the floor; but now, my greased legs stuck to the cold leather cushion. I shifted to the side and tried to slide a little closer to Romell—an attempt to snuggle on this sofa of his. The next thing I knew, the section I was sitting on tipped over; I had slipped. Friction between my skin and the leather caused a noise about as subtle as a blast from a whoopee cushion, and now, my body was wedged between the seats, caught in an entanglement of leather and elastic that was mashing my already sore breasts. I immediately looked up at Romell. I could tell this position was doing little for my sex appeal, but to make this seem less awkward, I flashed a smile. Romell didn't even crack one; so, ignoring the pain in my breasts, I struggled free and made myself comfortable on the floor where he soon joined me.

"You seem to be feeling better," he said.

"Not yet," I said. I unbuttoned my shorts, zipped them down, and let out a sigh of relief.

He straightened and inched away. "What are you doing?"

"The shorts are tight. I could hardly breathe." That was an honest answer, but Romell still cut his eye at me suspiciously for a moment. Then he wrung his hands; his shoulders relaxed as he leaned forward. Through the fabric of his tight, white tank, the tiered muscles in his back were clearly defined. I sipped a breath and hissed. Romell whipped his head around. Now, his eyes were on me, so I sniffled. "Romell," I said. I then inhaled, releasing a deep sigh. "Why don't you play some music?"

He picked the stereo remote off the marble cocktail table. "What's good?" he asked.

I thought about our conversation at Pookie's Jukebox and smiled. I answered, "'Right Here'? 'Downtown'."

He responded quickly. "Chocolate, I'm not even going there with you. Not this time. Now, what do you wanna hear?"

I fought the urge to blurt the next thought that popped into my head: "*I Wanna Sex You Up.*" Instead, I said something a little more subtle, "You can play some Marvin Gaye, Romell. 'I Want You'."

He shook his head, clicked the remote, and the ballad, "Dry Your Eyes," filled the room in stereo-surround sound. Swaying with the music, I eased my way to Romell's side, snuggled up, and rested my head on his shoulder.

The instant I wrapped my arm around his waist, he shut the power off and I slapped my own thigh in frustration. "Why'd you turn it off?" I shouted.

Once again, he inched away. "That's all you need to hear."

We locked eyes. I batted my lashes, moistened my lips, and panted, "I know The Deele."

"Yeah?" Romell snapped, "Then, you also know 'Two Occasions' played out." He tightened his lips. "You turned me down! Remember? Now, what do you want from me?"

Obviously, my subtlety wasn't working. Since he was challenging me to be direct, I obliged. "I want some TLC. 'Ain't Too Proud to Beg.' How about 'If I

Was Your Girlfriend?' Hell, right now, I really want the 'Red Light Special!' "

"Stop it, Chocolate." He looked away, hung his head, and pressed a button on his remote. The song that played this time was the a cappella version of "If I Ever Fall in Love."

I sucked my teeth. "Oh! So, now you wanna play Shai!"

He giggled, but his eyes were moist when he looked back at me. "Mia, take your ass home."

Wow. My eyes brimmed with tears. These were real. "I can't go home now."

Now he looked into my eyes. I was sure he noticed my tears, but still he shook his head, pointed to the door, and said, "Take your ass somewhere else; that's up to you, but you can't stay here." He stood up and cocked his head to the side. I waited for him to give me the fuck-you nod, but he didn't. So, for a moment, I just stared at his silhouette against the backdrop of his charcoal walls. Then, I focused on the bridge of his nose and his moistened lips that were now pursed in aggravation. I looked down, and I paid particular attention to his muscles, noting the pattern of the veins in his arm and shoulder. The cotton tank, stretching across the expanse of his chest, was on the verge of bursting at the seams, but it hung loosely at his waistline, revealing his dark brown flesh and the silky hairs that were always visible right over the elastic of this particular pair of cotton shorts. *He's not wearing underwear, again, but that doesn't matter.* I sighed and continued to record his every detail down to the grey carpet fibers between his toes. Then, I looked back into Romell's squinted eyes. He scratched his head and said, "What?"

My answer was solemn. "Nothing." This was the second time he made me feel like two cents. I started to say so. But now, that didn't matter, either. I stood, grabbing my purse and slowly walked toward the door. "Goodbye, Romell. Thanks for being *such* a good friend."

"Don't take this the wrong way," he said.

Without turning around, I said, "Too late for that now."

When There's No Wins...

*H*OW ELSE WAS I SUPPOSED TO TAKE IT? LIKE I told Romell, I couldn't go home. I couldn't go home now or ever again. Nothing would be the same. There was nothing there for me now. I had failed...at everything. I stepped through the double glass doors of the sky lounge into the moist heat outside and took a good look. Scattered clouds stretched through the evening sky like tulle. In the still wind, somehow all drifted southeast—all, except a dense plume looming above. My heels clicked with each step across the paved walkway, until I reached the stone fire pit at the other end. The sun was long gone, and there were no stars; the moon was nowhere to be seen. Even searching the clouds, I didn't see any blurred circle of light or any portion of the moon, just darkness. Off in the distance as far as I could see, more darkness was closing in, making the flattened skyline of Queens resemble an industrial graveyard.

I took a deep breath, inhaling muggy air seasoned with salt from the East River. Then, I kicked my shoes off and knelt on top of the fire pit, hoisting myself up to get a better view over the concrete wall. My heart felt like it was twice as large; it was exploding out of my chest in heavy thumps that throbbed even more than my now rock-hard breasts. The porous concrete felt scratchy against my arms, but bracing myself, I peered all the way down. There were no obstructions. It would be a straight drop. I returned to my feet, picked up my pumps, and took a deep breath. Now, it was time to work up the nerve to do this.

I stepped out of the shadows toward a lounge chair that sat directly beneath a lamppost a few feet away. There, in the light, I dropped my pumps and then sat on the edge of the chair's beige cushion. Reaching into my carryall, I immediately pulled out a pen; I had to fish around for paper. Feeling everything else—my wallet, tangled headphone wires, keys, the plastic bags from the record store Romell and I went to—I didn't feel one scrap of paper. All I needed was a tiny piece. I looked into one of the plastic bags, hoping it had a receipt in it among the CDs. It did. I pulled it out, placing it on my thigh. I was about to scribble on the front, until I took a look at it. Strangely, it had an itemized list of titles that caught my attention: *Ready to Die, Xscape, Jump, Right Here.* How appropriate. I paused for a moment then looked up. With a deep breath, I mumbled, "I just can't believe this is the end." That said, I flipped the receipt over to the back and began to write. My pen moved across the tiny white square leaving a teeny, blue ink trail of script to mark my last words:

So much for today
There is no tomorrow
Too many mistakes
And too much sorrow
Why should I fight
When I can't win
I just can't believe this is the end

Those tiny words trailed all the way down to the bottom, all the way to the very corner. I flipped the receipt back to the front and read the itemized list once again: *Ready to Die, Xscape, Jump, Right Here.* My hand started shaking. I reached back into my

44

carryall for the other receipt. I needed to write something that would serve as my will. I fumbled around inside the next plastic bag. Pinned beneath a shrink-wrapped, jewel case, there it was—the tiny slip of paper. I pulled it out and placed it on my thigh. My mind drew a blank. And then, I realized I didn't own anything worth anything. My whole wardrobe was outdated. I only wore costume jewelry and sterling silver, and every stitch of furniture I owned came from a thrift store. I took a deep breath and flipped the receipt over. There was an itemized list there, too. I couldn't believe what it said. In laser sharp text were two titles in this order: *Keep on Moving, Back to Life*. That was strange. A tear rolled down my cheek. I flipped that slip of paper from side to side in disbelief, over and over again as if the printing would somehow change. *Was this a sign?* I flipped both receipts, now rereading all sides. Romell bought these CDs back in the record store. We were talking about these very same songs earlier. I closed my eyes, trying to convince myself that this was a coincidence.

I pulled my CD player out of the bag and put on my headphones. I stuffed the two receipts into the inside pocket of my carryall bag, stood, took a deep breath, and walked barefoot toward the fire pit. Then, I reached inside my bag for some exit music—the one CD that would surely urge me to do this: "Jump." I fumbled through the CDs in my carry all; I didn't see it. I turned around and sat back down on the lounge chair. I stared up into the sky, but still didn't see one star. The cloud over me was not moving. I took another deep breath. Dumping the contents of my purse, I now searched for "Jump" or "Back to Life." Either one would make up my mind one way or the other, but neither was in the bag. I shook my head.

Standing back up, I reached over to the potted tree behind the chair. It looked like a small pine, but it was trimmed in such a way that the branches spiraled up. I pulled the carryall off my shoulder and hung it onto the tree. Then, I picked up the *Ready to Die* CD. Peeling plastic wrap away from the jewel case, I noticed the picture of the baby on the front. "Why in the hell would they put a baby on the cover of a CD called 'Ready to Die'? That is sick and twisted!" I stared at it. He was such a big, beautiful baby. Huge Afro. I smiled. My little Tee-Bo was still scrawny, long but scrawny, and I was supposed to be his next meal. My tears came again. I grabbed my purse and planted myself on the chair's cushion.

Okay, so now I wouldn't do anything stupid, but I still wasn't ready to go home just yet, so I snapped "Keep on Moving" into my CD player. Funny, I always thought the title was "Keep *It* Moving." I shook my head and turned the volume way up. I was wrong about the title, so instead of getting lost in the bass line once again, I paid attention to the words.

I didn't even know those CDs were in my bag before, but I listened to this song now. The words were so uplifting; I wished I paid attention to them sooner. As soon as I heard Soul II Soul sing the lyrics, "*Find your own way to stay,*" I completely burst into more tears.

Still I Want You With Me...

*M*Y BATTERIES DIED. I DON'T KNOW EXACTLY
when I fell asleep, but it was a cold, wet
drop on my forehead that woke me. I smeared it from
my face, wiped my eyes clear, and opened them,
facing west. I gave myself a good stretch and noticed
how the sky's once deep, dark blue faded into grayish
purple clouds and then this band of red in the east. I
took my headphones off and stood. Across the river, I
saw the sun. Emerging through the crimson tint, it
was orange. With each passing moment, it became
brighter and brighter. This was the first time I'd ever
seen a sunrise and right now, Queens looked like
heaven. Nothing mattered but these colors on the
horizon. Only God could make something this
beautiful. It was then that I realized: when I came
into this world I didn't have Spider or Romell, and
when I leave this world I won't have Spider or Romell.
More and more drops hit me, but this was the
thought that was on my mind as I stood there
watching a canopy of light rise and the sun disappear
into the haze. Eventually, I looked down. Cool drops
speckled my arms. Light rain also speckled my bare
feet. Up above me, the clouds were dense. The air
was only a tad cooler than it had been the night
before, but a strong wind appeared out of nowhere,
and I could actually see it blow; dust, gum wrappers,
and cigarette butts gathered into a vortex of debris
that swirled high and swept across the roof deck. And

47

then I heard the crack of thunder. This was going to be a heavy downpour. I shielded my spiral curls with my arm, gathered my things, and made tracks back inside.

Not even two minutes later, I had my key in Romell's cylinder. I unlocked it and tipped in. I was only stopping in for an umbrella. Romell had an umbrella stand in his hall closet. It was tall and ebony with hand-carved, tribal warriors. His closet was all the way past his living room near his bedroom. I walked to the back quietly. The wheels of the closet's mirrored door squeaked in their track as I slid it open. Romell's umbrella stand had only one bleached wooden handle extending from it. I pulled the umbrella out; it was pink with a D&G logo etched into a metal plate on the handle. One of his girlfriends must've left it. I put it to the side, reached my arm all the way down inside the wooden tube, and felt around the bottom. There was nothing else in there, so I decided to check his closet floor. I got down on my hands and knees and fumbled around for a moment, seeing only galoshes, suitcases, a few Barron's and Pass Perfect study guides, Romell's gym bag, his briefcase, and his laptop—no umbrella. So, I backed my way out, stood, and then slid the closet door closed. In the mirror, I saw Romell behind me, bare-chested and dumbfounded, whispering, "What are you doing here?"

"I was looking for an umbrella," I said. "I found one, so now, I'm leaving."

"You can't take that one."

"The hell I can't!"

"Shhh! Lower your voice."

"Why are you whispering?"

"I have company."

My jaw dropped. Then, I whispered, "Who?"

"Akasma."

"That snooty bitch!"

Romell grabbed me by the elbow and whisked me

through the living room all the way to the passageway by the front door. I shook my arm out of his grasp. "You trifling Negro."

"Why am I trifling?"

"You wasted no time gettin' that bitch up in here."

"Don't stand here and call Akasma names. You don't even know her."

"I know who she is! She's the one with the long, dark, wavy hair and the cleft in her chin; she wears the six-inch, patent leather pumps and Chanel sunglasses. The flight attendant. I know exactly who she is. She was coming to visit you once and saw me leaving your apartment. She asked me if I worked for you! She's snooty! At least Jun Ko's friendly! Jun Ko's a genuinely nice girl; I can understand why you'd want to be with *her*!"

"Wait a minute! You hate Jun Ko, too!"

Now, I couldn't look at him. He had every reason to believe that. I backed against the wall, folding my arms across my chest. "I don't *hate* Jun Ko. She's a nice girl," I grunted.

Romell stood in front of me. "If Jun Ko's such a nice girl, why don't you like her?"

"I have nothing against Jun Ko."

"Chocolate, any time I mention her name your whole demeanor changes. Now, tell me why."

I squeezed away from him. "I don't know, Romell." Hanging the umbrella's handle on my arm, I swung his door open. "You're smart. You figure it out."

In the hall, dragging my feet across the tweed carpeting to the elevator, I was in tears. To make matters worse, Romell stepped into the hall behind me, even though he was barefoot and wearing nothing but paisley, silk boxers. He looked at me with sad, sorry eyes and said, "Chocolate."

I wiped the blur from mine and looked at him. "What?" I said.

"That's Akasma's umbrella."

I looked at the logo on the handle. "Dolce. It

figures." Now, even more tears welled up in my eyes and spilled over, running down my face. I stiffened my quivering lips and handed Romell the umbrella.

"Chocolate, why are you crying?"

"I'm crying, because I feel like two cents *waitin'* for change." I turned away and smacked the down button. Then, shook my head and began to chuckle.

Romell drew a deep breath. "Now, why are you laughing?"

"I'm laughing, because this is the third time you made me feel like two cents waiting for change, and you still haven't paid me my dollar."

"I don't owe you a dollar."

The elevator door opened, I stepped inside, and turned around. "Yes, you do."

"No, I don't, because if I owed you anything, I would have given it to you."

I pressed the lobby button and rolled my eyes at him. The doors were closing just as I said, "Wanna bet?"

In the elevator I sucked my teeth. The noise was so loud; it triggered a letdown reflex. Milk leaked into my bikini top and seeped through my transparent tank in wet, pink circles. I folded my arms across my chest until I'd rushed through the lobby and out of the building into the dim, early-morning light and the hot, salty breeze. Overhead, dark clouds ruffled the sky.

I hurried to the corner. *That was dumb; coming to Romell's was a dumb move. Why would I even try to jump from a man who doesn't believe in marriage to a man who doesn't even believe in relationships? That was stupid. Stupid. Stupid. Stupid.* The rain began to come down harder as I stood there flailing my arm to hail a taxi. I heard thunder. My once crisp spiral curls were now drooping. I reached into my carryall for one of the record store's plastic bags as that was to be my only head cover. The plastic bag ripped when I pulled it out. I grunted in absolute frustration, threw my carryall to the ground. *I don't know why I didn't go over that wall.* No sooner had that thought entered my mind than I heard the burst of thunder and the clouds opened and dumped on me. Not a sprinkle or a drizzle, this was torrential, whipping through the air in horizontal patterns; I was almost drowning in it. In an instant, First Avenue was a river, and both empty and occupied taxis whizzed by, plowing through. Now, I snatched up my carryall and reached for the only plastic bag I had left. Just as I shook it out to lay it over my head, I heard a screech and looked up; a taxi from the center lane swerved and skidded to an abrupt stop right in front of me with a splash. Nasty, dirty street water was in my eyes, all up my nose, and all in my mouth. And, what was left of my spiral curls was now sliding down my back in waves. I stamped my feet and hollered, "Oh, I'll be—"

I'm Hanging On...

*O*KAY. *I NEED TO START WATCHING WHAT I SAY.*
It dawned on me. Mommy warned me
several times to stop saying, "I can't live without
Spider." The problem was not only did I continue to
say it, but I also believed that, just like I believed I
couldn't live without Romell. That's what compelled
me to do the things I did that led me all the way up to
the roof of Romell's building. I once thought I had it
all together. Everyone else seemed to be the problem:
Spider was cold; Romell, superficial; Mommy,
overbearing, Dawn, gossipy. Now, I recognized what
was wrong with my life was not the fault of Dr.
Snyder and Jackie, Mommy and Dawn, or even
Spider and Romell; it was a direct result of my own
thoughts and actions. I made my own decisions.
There was no one to blame but me. *I* needed to
change. I needed to change what I said and did
because I *didn't* have it all together. If being on that
roof deck brought me nothing else, it brought clarity.

Riding home in the taxi that had just splashed the
hell out of me, I was a puddle, but I thought about
what was right in my life. Spider had his way of being
cold and inconsiderate, but he stayed with me, and
there were many times when he had every reason not
to. Romell was cocky and superficial, but if he and I
never spoke again in life, I would still have a lifetime
of memories to smile about. My sister—pain in the
ass that she was—would always tell my secrets;
however, there was never a problem I presented to

53

Dawn that she didn't try to help me solve in one way or another. Dawn couldn't keep a secret, but she would always have my back. And, even though Mommy was overbearing, I never once doubted her love. And nobody was as on point with advice as she was. So, my sister's adage was right—Mommy *was* almost always right, and she ain't never lied.

Water was still dripping off of me when I stepped into my living room. I didn't change out of my wet, nasty clothes; I didn't sit down. Before I did anything, I plugged my phone back into the jack and called Mommy. Once I heard her voice, I immediately apologized. "I'm sorry, Mommy. I'm sorry for hanging up on you. I was under a lot of stress."

"I knew you had to be if you could get flip and hang up on *me* like that."

"And I'm also sorry for not listening when I should have. You were right."

"What's wrong?"

"Why?"

"You sound like you were crying."

I hadn't shed a tear since I left Romell's. How she could still sense that I had been crying was beyond me. I took a deep breath. "I had a rough night, Mommy. Spider and I broke up."

"I am sorry to hear that. Do you want to talk about it?"

"Not now. I'll talk to you about it later, but you *were* right."

Mommy sighed. "Mia, I don't tell you what I tell you so that I can be right. I want the best for you. That's why I'm still upset about you not graduating, not because I wanted to show off. I rented a car and drove six hours in the rain to get to D.C., and when I got there and saw you were in the audience with me instead of on stage getting your diploma, I was flabbergasted. I'm still flabbergasted."

"Yeah, I know. I'm sorry."

"And I'm sorry for slapping you," she said. "That

was uncalled for. But, try to understand: I've made too many mistakes in *my* life to raise a couple of fools."

Tears trickled down my cheeks. Now, I could see how she felt, and I understood why Mommy was so full of unsolicited advice. Experience brings lessons, and if nothing else, our mistakes make us experts on the subject of what not to do. After all I'd just been through, if I saw Tee-Bo on the verge of making some of the same mistakes I made, I would be just as unrelenting as she was. I wiped away my tears, and I sniffled quietly, but nothing got past Mommy. "Are you okay, Mia?"

I could hear the concern in her voice. "I'm fine now," I insisted, but I wasn't fully convinced myself, so I knew I had to cut *this* conversation short. "Talk to you later, Mommy. I wanna catch Dawn before she heads out."

"I wouldn't call her if I were you."

"Why not?"

"She's a little upset with you right now."

Now, I was confused. "What did *I* do?"

Mommy chuckled and said, "Right after you hung up, I called Dawn and asked her what the hell you were talking about, so Dawn went on to explain how soon Kyle is supposed to be getting his divorce. She rambled on for about twenty minutes, before I let in that you never told me Kyle was married."

"Ooh!" I giggled. "She told on herself, huh?"

"Yeah, so I'm warning you; if you call her for any reason before her brooding period is up, expect to get cussed out."

"Understood. I guess I'll have to wait to apologize to *her*. Love you, Mommy."

"One more thing, Mia. How did you get Tee-Bo's rash to go away?"

"The rash?"

"Yeah. What did you do for it?"

"There's a method with quite a few steps. Why?"

"It's back, and Carole said cornstarch isn't working. So, you'll either have to explain to her how to get rid of it, or go get him and take care of it yourself."

I sighed. "No problem, I'll pick him up tomorrow night after work. I might even pick him up tonight. Either way, I'll call Aunt Carole later and let her know for sure. I'll take care of it, Mommy."

"I know you will. I'll talk to you later, Mia. Call me if you need me."

After Mommy hung up, I sat there on my leather chair for a minute with both hands at my temples. *Man. I had totally forgotten to tell Aunt Carole what to do for Tee-Bo's skin. Dawn was right; I was stressed. Normally, my main concern is Tee-Bo. Lately, it seems like Tee-Bo's the last thing on my mind. And to think, I was even contemplating suicide.* I shook my head. *I'll never do that again. I don't care what I'm going through. I will tough it out, because if my life is for no other purpose, it's to be Tee-Bo's mother.* Thinking about that, I had to admit; despite all the breastfeeding, diaper changing, and all around caregiving, the reality of me being a mother never fully sank in. Somehow, it still wasn't real to me. But I had to think of it this way: as much as I craved Mommy's attention growing up, now, Tee-Bo deserved mine.

I don't like to think about it or talk about it, but I used to reach into the medicine cabinet and take some of Mommy's pills. I took the very first Humphrey pill because I thought they were vitamins. It made me burp for like fifteen minutes straight. After a while, I felt nauseous, my stomach knotted up real tight, and began to cramp. And then, the room felt like it was spinning. My stomach started retching, and I was gulping back this bitter taste until I couldn't hold it down anymore. I thought my stomach was empty, but I threw up anyway, and when I did, I saw what looked like yellow paint. That was bile, a taste I'll never forget. To this day, I think bile is the worst taste ever. But, when Mommy came home, she came straight into my room, sat on the edge of my bed, and put my head on her lap, rubbing my back and telling me everything was going to be okay. I forgot all about that bitter taste and remembered the attention I got. She asked me what I ate for lunch, and I told her, but I didn't mention a thing about that pill. And since I knew the pills wouldn't kill me, every now and then, I'd pop another one, two, sometimes three. Dawn always thought I was faking, but was convinced I was bulimic after watching some ABC Afterschool Special. But I was already skinny. I wasn't trying to make myself skinnier. Really, I just loved the fact that the chaos of everyday life would stop. I'd stay home from school, and Mommy would take off from work just for me. And when I'd stop puking, Mommy would make me ginger tea steeped from the actual root and a bowl of stewed chicken and noodles. And I loved stewed chicken and noodles. I think as a result of taking those pills, I got my first period two years before Dawn got hers, and she's three and a half years older. At ten years old, seeing blood in the toilet, I thought those pills burned a hole in my intestines. Mommy and I hadn't had "the talk" yet, so I called Romell first, thinking I was dying. Hysterical, I told him all about the Humphreys, and that I didn't want to die. I was only taking them to make myself sick for a little while. After the scare was over, he made me promise not to do "that" again. He never labeled it, but he still treated me like the least little thing that upset me would have me reaching for pills.

Anyway, that's something I chose to put behind me, but if getting attention was that important to me, I really should've been more mindful of Tee-Bo. He should've been my main concern. Instead of what was really the case, wanting to hurt Romell as badly as I felt he hurt me. There I was ready to throw myself off a building, and he called the next woman over. And, after the worst night of my life, Romell threw me out into the pouring rain, and left me ass-out with no umbrella. But, men will be men. I couldn't concern myself with Romell or who he decided to sleep with. My sole purpose was not for me to be here for Romell or Spider. It was time for me to worry about my son. Life is much too precious.

My crocodile pumps were cold and soaked down to the soles. I kicked them off and snatched them up by the heels. Making my way down the hall, my damp feet slapped against my old, wood floor. As soon as I approached the bathroom, I caught a whiff of that apricot oil along with something musty. I tried not to look, but couldn't help sneaking a peek anyway. The bathroom rug was soaked, so it was wet rubber I smelled. My clothes were still on the floor where I dropped them; makeup was all over the place. What disgusted me most was a soggy bar of Ivory soap still floated atop bathwater murky with soap scum, because I didn't bother to drain the tub before I left. I shook my head. That task was too overwhelming right now.

But, I was even more overwhelmed when I pushed my bedroom door open. I stepped over my towel into the room. Belts and scarves, panties and bras—everything was everywhere. I had forgotten I'd left in such a rush. Then, I looked into the mirror. The makeup was completely washed off my face. Through my tank top, my pink bikini was totally visible, as were my hard nipples. And, my spiral curls...I gave my hair a squeeze and water just ran from them. I looked like I'd just returned from Claremont Pool after being thrown in fully dressed. I flung my carryall to the floor. *I'm a mess. This place is a mess. There's no way I'm going to work today. That agency could write me up if they wanted to. At this point, I don't even care if they put me on suspension; I hate bill collecting, anyway.*

With a sigh, I brushed the heap of underwear away and flopped my soggy ass down onto the edge of my bed. I looked from the crib Spider originally assembled lopsided, to his record player in the corner knocked on its side, and to all my bras lying in disarray. Cologne bottles were everywhere. There was no way I could clean this mess and not think of Spider or Romell. Besides that, I felt nasty. There was this layer of grit on my face, so first things first.

After I washed my face, I peeled off my top, the shorts, and my bathing suit. Then, I reached for the one thing that was sure to make me feel better—my poetry journal. I turned to a clean page, unzipped the inside pocket of my carryall and pulled out the two receipts. They were damp. The ink was smudged, but they were still legible. Line by line, I neatly copied the words from the first receipt into my journal.

> *So much for today*
> *There is no tomorrow*
> *Too many mistakes*
> *And too much sorrow*
> *Why should I fight?*
> *When I can't win*
> *I just can't believe this is the end*

Raising my pen to the top margin, I scribbled in the title, *I Just Can't Believe This Is the End*. The structure for this poem seemed so familiar. I moistened my middle finger and flipped to the last poem. Sure enough, it was very similar. I read to the ending.

> *Please show me*
> *What I don't see*
> *What's the reason?*
> *4 the problem*

Strangely, that poem was entitled, *Is This the*

Beginning of the End. The poem I just wrote I titled, *I Just Can't Believe This Is the End.* That was so strange. There almost seemed to be a connection. I moistened my fingertip again and now flipped through all the pages. The titles seemed to be in a sequence that spelled out almost exactly what I'd been going through for the past few days. *Believe, It's Just a Matter of Time, Chocolate Love, Is This the Beginning of the End, I Just Can't Believe This Is the End.*

It was as if somewhere, deep down inside, I was predicting what was going to happen. I knew I was going to consider ending my life. Last night and since then, there had been a series of coincidences—the titles on the receipts just so happened to fall in an order that made sense; they also happened to reflect my own thoughts at the time. When I was looking for the "Jump" CD to play as my very last song that was not in the bag, and now the order of my very own poems. What was strange was how all this just so happened to fall into place right after Romell and I did our play on song titles in the record store and how all this also happened to fall into place right before I considered suicide.

Maybe this was all a coincidence. But then again, what if everything happens for a reason? If this wasn't an accident or a coincidence, what does this all mean? For once, I didn't have the answers. I didn't know what to make of any of this, but I knew who would be the right person to ask.

$\mathscr{F}_{or}$ $\mathscr{D}_{ear}$ $\mathscr{L}_{ife}$...

ITTING ON MY BED, I PICKED UP MY PHONE. THEN I shook my head and placed it back. I took a deep breath and exhaled. I felt uneasy; my stomach was churning like a taffy machine. I laughed. "I've got to get a grip." I took another breath and slowly released it. Somewhere from outside, through the downpour, I heard a running motor rumble. There was a hiss and then the squeak of brakes. After what seemed like only seconds later, I heard the grinding of gears and clattering between the hum of hydraulics. Now, I knew it was a garbage truck. The Department of Sanitation is always prompt. Even in this nasty weather, I could set my watch to them. Now, back to the matter at hand, I picked the phone up, grunted, and placed it back down, looking around me, but searching for nothing. I was stalling, and I knew it. I had an idea of what I wanted to say, but still, this wasn't easy. Especially since I had been avoiding her. *Maybe I shouldn't even call.* I only reconsidered for a split second, because I glanced at my journal and saw that title again, *I Just Can't Believe This Is the End.* I snatched up my phone and dialed. On the first ring, Mrs. Goodwin picked up. "Good morning," she said. Hearing her gentle voice, I smiled, and my eyes grew misty.

Now, after all the times I ducked her so I wouldn't have to go to church, after taking her for granted for so long, and even though I had yet to read a single Bible verse she recommended, here I was being comforted by the mere sound of her voice. Still, my own voice trembled when I said, "Hello."

"What's wrong?" she said.

"I just had the worst night of my life."

"Well, Mia. Weeping may endure through the night, but joy comes in the morning."

I took a deep breath and then I asked, "Mrs. Goodwin, how do we know if God is trying to tell us something?"

"God is always trying to tell us something. That's why we should read our Bibles so that we can know exactly what He says. Have you opened that brand-new Bible of yours yet?"

"No, I haven't."

"Why haven't you?"

"I don't know. No, I do. Mrs. Goodwin, I didn't know if I believed or not until this morning. Now, I think I do."

"Well, Sweetheart. That's something you definitely need to make up your mind about. You give that some thought, and I'll keep praying for you."

"You'll *keep* praying for me?"

"Yes, Mia. I've always been praying for you. You've been on my mind a lot lately, so I've been praying for you more than usual."

I didn't know how to respond to that. "Thank you," I said uneasily, then added, "Romell *has* been telling me to call you for some time. When I finally spoke to you, one thing you said was absolutely right."

"What's that?"

"All relationships *do* go through changes. Love changes. First, it's hot. Then, it's cold. It goes through its ups and downs, back and forth. You love 'em one moment and hate 'em the next. So, I can't take it anymore. I give up."

"Mia, love—as we understand it—changes, because we change. But, God is God all the time. He never changes. God's love remains the same, and His love endures forever," she said. My eyes started tearing. I wiped them dry and sniffled quietly. But then, Mrs. Goodwin asked, "Are you going to work today?"

"No," I sighed, "I don't feel up to it. Why do you ask?"

"Why don't you come to church with me? Midday service starts at noon."

"Not today, Mrs. Goodwin."

"Okay, Mia. Call me at work if you change your mind. And think about what I said, because living in this world unsure about your beliefs is like the love of your life and your soul mate being two different people."

Hearing her say "two different people," I was now afraid of where this conversation would lead. Quickly, I said, "Well, I don't have that problem. I have to go now. I'm late for work. I'll talk to you later. Bye."

I didn't mean to hang up on her, but it seemed she was leading up to asking me about my feelings for Spider *and* Romell. Still, hanging up on her wasn't right, I knew better. *She didn't deserve that.*

I opened my night table drawer. Light hit the gold words embossed on the spine, New International Version. I reached in and pulled out my Bible. As I opened it up, the crisp, clean pages crackled. A receipt fell out. It was from the Salvation Army. *What on earth did I buy from the Salvation Army? Oh, yeah, the CD player.* The receipt was impressed with my own handwriting on the reverse side. I flipped it over and read it. John 3:16, Isaiah 54:10, and Psalm 119:41—those were the verses Mrs. Goodwin had given me. I moistened my middle finger. Snatching back the flimsy pages, I ripped a couple, but I found the first verse. "For God so loved the world that he gave his one and only Son, that whoever believes in him shall not perish but have eternal life" (John 3:16). And, the next one, "Though the mountains be shaken and the hills be removed, yet my unfailing love for you will not be shaken nor my covenant of peace be removed, says the Lord, who has compassion on you" (Isaiah 54:10). And, the last, "May your unfailing love come to me, O LORD, your salvation according to your promise" (Psalm 119:41).

This all seems well and good, but I'm still not sure. Mrs. Goodwin says living in the world unsure about your beliefs is like the love of your life and your soul mate being two different people. Maybe that's the case, but I don't have that problem. I don't have Spider; we broke up. And, if Romell and I can't be lovers, then we can't be friends, so I don't have him either. I may have thought Spider was the love of my life, but Romell definitely was never, is never, and will never be my soulmate.

Nothing's Working...

I DON'T WANNA BE WITH ROMELL. DIMES—THAT'S
all he wants. Dimes. I'm worth so much more,
but Romell's so superficial; he doesn't see that. And, in
a span of not even two full days, he went from Jun Ko
to me and then to Akasma. And, Jun Ko's ass went
running to his room with whipped cream. And, he put
me out in the rain, too! Oh, I'll never speak to Romell's
ass again. And as for Spider, when we broke up, he
didn't cry, scream, cuss, yell, none of that. He just left.
He was only mildly disappointed after ten years of us
being together. Ten whole years. If that man cared
about me, he would have been crushed. I'd bet any
amount of money that he's lying up with some other
bitch right now. If Romell and Spider can't see a good
thing staring them in the face, then Romell can kiss
one cheek and Spider can kiss the other. It's as simple
as that. I don't know why I believed Spider. Having a
baby for a man who's against marriage is a no-no.
And, for the life of me, I can't figure out why I allowed
myself to have that little crush on Romell. Getting
involved with a man who can't even commit to a
relationship is a definite no-no. Well, at least I learned
my lesson. So now, I can forget about Spider. And
Romell. I don't want either one. I don't need them. I
just wish I could stop thinking about them.

Rather than focus on the negative, I made myself
busy. I showered, shampooed my hair, put it in four
big plaits, and tied it up. At the salon, Dawn had kept
the perm in so long; it burned and now my scalp was

scaly. But I didn't call my sister, bitchin'. Instead, I slipped on some rubber gloves and commenced to clean each room from top to bottom. That didn't take long. When I'm heated, I do everything faster, but faster isn't always better. I soon had my head in the oven, coughing from noxious fumes. Common sense should've told me: it's not wise to scrub an oven without proper ventilation. I cracked the windows, letting in some air. But, those toxins still got to me. Bad enough my scalp was itching, now I was gagging. Because of a surge of adrenaline, this black woman forgot: she is not superhuman. So, my adrenaline buzz wasn't doing me a bit of good. The problem was I couldn't help but focus on Spider and Romell. Well, I had enough of being pissed off. I tugged off my rubber gloves, brushed my sweaty hands down my lucky nightgown, snatched off my scarf, and scratched my scabs.

I needed more of a distraction. In the living room, I opened my console and turned to an easy listening station. "You Gotta Be." I smiled and left it there. *Now, that's what I'm talking about!* That was exactly what I needed. I sang that song with Des'ree. Then I heard a noise and looked across the room. It wasn't the bass, so I turned the music down and stood still, listening. I didn't hear anything. In these buildings, there was always some banging going on: somebody's hammer, the pipes, ceilings, or bad-ass kids roaming the halls because they couldn't play in the rain. I turned the music back up. It didn't sound like the door, but I walked over, slid the cover off the peephole, and checked just to be sure. No one was there, so I went back to cleaning.

The only thing left to do was the polishing. I started with my bachelor's chest and ended with my console, which I always gave so much more attention to. Mrs. Goodwin had the same one years ago. Maybe that's why I fell in love with it. One particular morning, it had been there just sitting by the garbage truck, but waiting for me. I brought it in, and Spider had a fit, understandably. The glass was broken, but this was good wood, and it was all pine. I had gotten so excited; I soon stripped it and had it up against the wall. Later, replacing the shattered mirror and all the panes cost me big time. But in the inlay, there's my happy reflection. In retrospect, the console was exactly what I wanted. Good thing I won Spider over. Only a fool would refuse such a nice piece because of a little broken glass.

Okay. All the wood was done, now it was time for that mirror over the loveseat. I grabbed that mirror off the wall but forgot how tedious this process was. Scrubbing the scrollwork with an old toothbrush was a pain in the ass. I loved this mirror because it was beautiful, a little old-fashioned, but that was its charm. Now, hanging it back on the wall, the mirror looked like I gave up on it. The frame was shiny, except for a little tarnish, but I just didn't have the desire to stick with it. I was beginning to think sterling silver was a lot like Spence Snyder, too much work.

My two crystal candlestick lamps only took a second. They had ridges, so it wasn't like the fingerprints were visible. I grabbed a paper towel and wiped them just to be wiping them. But that wasn't the case with my crystal centerpieces. No paper towels for these two. I polished them with a lint-free cloth. First, the decanter: sleek, with rounded shoulders and a nice stopper. Then the fluted vase, it stood a little higher, long and lean. Both centerpieces were cobalt blue, with no chips, cracks, or scratches, but the vase was a gorgeous piece of hand-blown glass.

I wiped my forehead and took a long, hard look. Spider was always so indifferent about everything I did, but we came here with nothing, moving into four empty rooms and an echo. Every time I brought in something shabby and made it chic, that was my little victory. My loveseat with its camel back, my chaise with its Queen Anne legs, this mix of texture and color: periwinkle walls, the wood, the mirror, pillows, leather, upholstery, and the crystal; in this room all the elements came together. Here was my proof that even though I made some bad decisions, something was right about me. *My place is beautiful, even if no one else appreciates it.*

All right, enough of this light stuff, time to change the pace. I opened the console and tuned my radio past the static to an old Funkadelics song. I listened closer, snapping my fingers, then turned it up. It was their music, but some female was singing about being a freak. *This is hot!* I couldn't help dancing, and as soon as I caught onto the words, I started singing too.

The artist was Adina Howard. I had just finished scribbling her name on the back of my *Modern Bride* magazine when I heard a tap. *I thought I heard something earlier. I'd bet any amount of money that's Jeff acting stupid. Why didn't he just ring the bell?* "Just a minute!" I turned the music down and looked out the peephole. Again, no one was there. "Who?" I said, pressing my ear to the cold door.

At first, there was a hum. Then, trying to listen closer through the paint, I heard nothing. "Who!" I still didn't hear anything. Now, I tightened my lips. "If this is Jeff, I'm going to cuss your ass out." I quickly unlocked my door, swung it open, and stepped over the threshold, screaming, "Jeff?" But, the long, bowlegs I saw down the corridor, approaching me in full swagger, weren't Jeff's.

Now I Don't Know

RAINWATER COVERED ROMELL'S HEAD. BEADS ran trails down his face. His jeans were soaked. Standing in front of me, he looked like a side of beef in his wet t-shirt. I kept staring. I always thought he didn't know where I lived, but then I remembered I mailed stuff to Romell, and I always wrote in the return address. I still couldn't believe I was seeing him. "How did you get here?"

He wiped his face with his bare hand. "The Jag's out front."

"You drove that convertible in this weather?"

"Top's up."

"Top's up? That car has never seen a speck of dust, let alone a raindrop. There's practically a monsoon out there."

"Shh! I need to talk to you, and I couldn't chance not catching a cab."

"Why didn't you call or wait until *I* called *you* like you always do?"

"I had to see you now."

"You just saw me a few hours ago."

He pulled my arm. "I need to talk to you."

"Okay, come inside."

"Nah, come down the hall with me. I need to talk to you...privately."

"Romell, if you want to talk to me privately, why are you asking me to come out into the hallway? Come inside."

He stepped back and looked at me. His eyebrows

drew together, and he squinted uneasily. "Is...is your man in there?"

"Spider is not my man!"

Romell cut his eye and tried to glance past me. I sucked my teeth. "No, Romell! He's not here! I told you last night that I put his ass out."

I backed into the apartment and held the door open. As soon as he stepped inside, I locked all four locks. When I turned, I saw he was in the middle of my living room. This was his first time here, but I didn't expect him to be looking around as if he were in a museum.

He walked over to my console. "This thing is solid. You're gonna have it for a long time." He knocked on the wood and turned around. "Your place is something, Chocolate. Who's your decorator?" I looked at him like he had a third eye. He looked back at me. It took a minute, but I saw the realization sink in; his eyes grew big, and for a moment, he couldn't stop blinking. He stepped to my chaise and stopped. Staring, he asked, "You don't have any idea how much this thing is worth, do you?"

"A lot I guess."

He responded, "If you need to guess, you *don't* know."

I shrugged, watching him shake his head and walk over to my loveseat, looking at everything again. Still in awe, he reached up to my crystal lamp and felt the blue silk lampshade. So I said, "Sometimes the most wonderful things fall right into our laps because someone else didn't appreciate them." For some reason, his head spun, and there was a strange look in his eyes that I couldn't read. Glancing away, I saw his Movado. The long hand was on the diamond and the short hand was where the ten should have been. "Romell, it's Thursday morning. Why aren't you at work?"

"I quit."

When he was begging me to stay yesterday, I

sensed something was bothering him. Now I knew what it was. "You what? When?"

"Yesterday, but nevermind that. Chocolate, you and I, we've been friends all our lives and—"

"Romell, you didn't have anything else lined up!" I moved around the living room. "Why on earth would you quit your job? How are you gonna manage?"

"I'll be fine. Look, Chocolate. You and I, we got something that—"

"Fine? Hello, Romell!" I walked up to him. "That *is* a Jaguar parked outside. Your bills ain't like mine!"

"Chocolate, trust me. I'll be fine. I saved for a rainy day. Now, what I've been trying to say is—"

"Saved for a rainy day?" I pulled the sheers aside, yanked the cord to the blinds, and pointed out the window to the storm raging outside. "Did you save for this? How much do you need?"

"I don't need to borrow anything! Trust me. I'll be fine." He looked away and then looked back at me, smiling. He moistened his lips and softened his voice, "And, I owe you now as it is."

I walked over to him. "You don't owe me any money."

"Yes I do."

"No, you don't!"

"Chocolate, I never welch on my wagers. And, we *did* agree that if I ever made you feel worthless, I'd owe you."

"Romell, we were nine-year-olds."

"A bet's a bet."

"You don't have to pay me, Romell. It is *not* that serious."

"Nah, it is to me." He grabbed my wrist, reached into the pocket of his jeans, and pulled out a closed fist. Slowly, he released ten cold dimes into the palm of my hand.

Standing there with this fist full of cold, wet dimes, I said, "What the hell is this?"

"A dollar."

"I can count! Why are you paying me in dimes?"

"I wanted to make a point."

I shook my head. "What point is that?"

"I don't want you to ever feel worthless, Chocolate, because for you, I'll gladly give up all my dimes."

I shrugged and my eyes searched his. "What are you saying?"

"Let me know right now what it is you want from me, whether it's friendship or a relationship, and I promise you: I will make that happen."

"Romell, you should know by now. I want a husband!"

"Whoa, Mia! Come on! I'm taking a big step here. Work with me! I've never done the relationship thing before, but I wanna give it a shot with you!"

I smiled and shook my head. "Relationship?" Then, I cut my eye at him. "With me? Don't you have enough women to choose from?"

"I want *you.*"

"What happened? Did Jun Ko run out of whipped cream? Did Akasma say you can't have any more of her Turkish Delights?"

"Chocolate, don't be like that. I only feel things when I'm with you."

"Oh really? So, I guess when Akasma was in your bed this morning, you weren't feeling things. And, when Jun Ko ran to your bedroom with that can of whipped cream, you didn't feel things then either, huh? Romell, take your ass home and flip through your Rolodex. Call somebody else. I got your number. You want all the comforts without the commitment. You're just as bad as Spider."

I headed for the door. When I reached for the knob, he grabbed my wrist and pulled me toward him.

"Mia! Look me in my eyes, and tell me you don't want me."

"I don't!"

He wrapped his arm around my waist and pulled

me into him. He was already hard. "Look me in the eye and say that again."

I dropped my head to hide my smile. "Romell, why are you putting me through this?"

"Chocolate, I don't wanna put you through anything; I just wanna be with you. I want *us* to be together."

I eased back, folded my arms across my chest, and looked into his eyes. "Well, I'll have to think about that."

He smiled; his dimples deepened—all three of them. "Tell you what, why don't you come by my place? *You* and *I* could do some thinking. We can go straight to my bedroom and think. Then, we can take a shower, grab a bite to eat, come back, and think some more. Take another shower, go and have dinner, and when we get back, we could think for the rest of the night. And, after all our thinking tomorrow morning, we could shower, and I'll bring you home."

I shook my head. "All these showers...for thinking?"

"Hey, you know me. I've got a dirty mind."

I giggled, even though that line sounded like something he was probably practicing for years. When I looked back into his eyes, he winked at me and I got the strangest feeling, like a tickle in the pit of my stomach. And then I heard the voices, rattling off all the reasons why I should be disgusted, reasons why Romell could never be what I needed, reasons why this was all wrong; Romell was wrong for me; I was wrong for him. But I closed my eyes, listening only to the rain and breathing in his scent. After clearing my mind of every thought and every fear, the only thing that mattered was how I felt about him. He made my heart swell, and now it was bigger than me. That's precisely why I did what I did next. I tiptoed in and brought my lips to his.

He turned his face away. "Did you have any peanuts today?"

73

"Nope."

"No peanut butter, either?"

I shook my head, nibbled his bottom lip and then, his top. My tongue found his and breath sweet from peppermint. Change slipped through my fingers and chimed, hitting the floor. I placed my hand under his wet shirt. His skin was cool and damp, but this was the first time I had ever consciously put my hand on any man other than Spider. I hissed and ran my hand up to his chest. It was just as hard as his abs. My other hand tried to pull his shirt off. He grabbed my wrist. I opened my eyes. "What's wrong?"

He shook his head. "What if your man comes back?"

"Spider's not my man, and he's not coming back." I closed my eyes and inched back up toward his lips. I felt him pull away. I sucked my teeth. "He's not coming back! And, even if he does, he can't get in because *I* have his keys!" Still hesitating, Romell looked at me. Then, slowly he brought his lips back to mine. The next thing I knew, we jostled from wall to wall, all the way up the hall, leaving a trail— Romell's shoes, t-shirt, and belt. We burst through my bedroom door, backing in, until I fell, pulling him onto the mattress. I kissed him again, but now, his soft lips stiffened. I opened my eyes and saw him glance sideways at the crib. "Come on, Romell."

"Nah, Mia. I think we should wait."

"Romell, don't stop now." I said. He turned away and shook his head. I softened my voice. "Come on. I know you want some of this hot Chocolate."

"He turned and there was that same look in his eyes he had when he was about to go down on me in the hallway. A jolt of fear shot to my stomach. He reached up under my nightgown, and in one snatch, ripped my panties clean off. He dropped them, dug into his pocket and stuck a condom in his mouth. He tore it open with his teeth and spat out the edge of the wrapper. He got up and turned his back to me.

His jeans dropped. I heard a faint crackle as the condom unraveled. And, before I could sneak a peek, he crawled over me. He reached down, probed me with his fingers and then, looked at them. I was so ready; those fingers were almost dripping. Romell stared into my eyes and eased himself inside.

Whoa. I took a sharp breath. Spider and I always fit together perfectly. This was different. This was definitely different. I could feel things shifting inside me. I exhaled in a slow whistle, and then, he started to move. "Wait!" I said.

"What's wrong?"

"Nothing. I just need a moment."

"A moment for what?"

"To brace myself." I looked into his eyes. He was still puzzled, so I added, "My garage is small, and your limo's a stretch."

He squinted. His eyes searched mine until they grew big, "Oh! Okay," he said half smiling. He dropped his face into my pillow. I felt him shake his head.

"Now, what's wrong with *you*?" I said.

"I can't." He looked over his shoulder at the crib. "This doesn't feel right to me."

"What? I can understand my discomfort, but what the hell is your complaint?"

"Not you! Us. Here. Now. I've got a bad feeling about this."

"Come on, Romell. Don't you want some of this?" He looked at me and shook his head again, but I was ripe. My heart, pounding louder than the tock-tick clock on my nightstand. I wrapped my arms around his waist. "Don't you want some Chocolate?"

"Nah, my instincts are never wrong. I know I tend to let my other head do the thinking, especially when I'm in this position." He looked at the clock, backed off, and sat on the edge of the bed, looking at the prom picture on the nightstand. "But not this time." He removed the condom and stuffed it in his pocket.

Then, he pulled his jeans on and buttoned them.

Right now, every part of me had a pulse. I jumped up and turned the prom picture facedown. Tugging at his jeans, I begged. I was squirming. "Come on, Romell. Don't you want some of this hot Chocolate?"

He smiled. "Sounds sweet. Can I have some whipped cream with that?" Then, he had the nerve to wink.

I caught a flashback of Jun Ko on her way to his bedroom. My lips immediately tightened. I pinched him. "Why do you always try to distract me?"

He shrugged. "It always works."

I smiled, but I was way past frustrated. Every single time the chance to make love to this man seemed to present itself, something managed to prevent it from happening. This was a pattern. And right now, all those years of anticipation, all that pent up sexual tension spilled out of me. He wiped my tears away with his thumb. "Chocolate, come on now. You know I hate to see you cry. Save those tears for a rainy day."

"It *is* raining." I sniffled. "Maybe this is just not meant for us. You and I will never have sex, Romell."

"What was this?"

I shrugged. "I wanted this all my life." I laughed and wiped away another tear. "So of course, something has to go wrong. Something *always* goes wrong. Things like this never happen to me. Good things happen for everyone else, but they never fucking happen for me! I don't know if it's my luck, fate, destiny, bad karma or worse. I'm cursed. That has to be it. Why else would—"

"Stop it! Stop talking crazy!"

"It'll never happen! Watch!"

"Yes, it will!"

"It didn't a minute ago! It didn't last night!"

He sighed, "Last night was something different. Look, Chocolate. Sooner or later, that man is coming back here. If for nothing else, he'll be back to pick up his things."

The concern I heard in his voice brought me back. I asked, "When did you start caring about Spider?"

"I don't give a damn about him. I care about *you*. That's why when you and I get together, I wanna be sure you don't have any regrets."

I looked at him and sighed. Then, I nodded.

He zipped his jeans and said, "Put something on, and come with me back to my place. We'll pick up right where we left off. I promise."

I smiled. "All right, but I'm gonna need a minute to get myself together."

He looked back at the clock. "Chocolate, it's pouring outside, just throw anything on. Your clothes are coming right off as soon as I get you to my place, anyway."

I twirled my finger around one of my plaits. "I am *not* going anywhere with my hair looking like this!"

"Okay, okay." He shook his head. "Just hurry up. I'll wait for you downstairs."

"Hold up, I'll walk you to the door." I stood, straightened my nightgown, and slipped on my fuzzy pink slippers. After removing the foiled edge of the condom wrapper from my bed, I then did a quick scan. Not seeing the larger piece, I crumpled the one I had and tossed it in the wastebasket. I stepped into the hall and watched him buckle his belt. He had already slid his feet into his shoes. He reached down, picked up his t-shirt, and pulled it over his head. Then, he took my hand, and our fingers locked. We stood there for a moment, just staring at each other. As we stepped into the living room, Romell looked around again. This time, he was nodding.

So I said, "I didn't need to buy a twenty-six thousand dollar sofa, either. I did my whole apartment for under a thousand dollars."

"Furniture, too?"

"Everything."

"I'm impressed. This is quaint, almost as cute as

you are, if that's possible. I still don't see why you won't let anybody help you out. Your mom is a furniture buyer. Miss Anne could've gotten brand-new furniture...at cost. And, you definitely could have gotten a bigger place somewhere else. If you needed a down payment or something, all you had to do was ask me. Instead, you chose to be stubborn. You do know you're stubborn, right?"

I shrugged. "Just a little bit."

Staring into my eyes, he gave me a gentle kiss on the back of my hand. Then he squeezed it to his heart. "I wouldn't change you for the world."

When he said that, I looked away feeling myself blush. A mousy sound came out of my mouth when I spoke. "You go ahead to the car. I'll be right down."

He gave me a peck on the lips. "Make it quick," he said and peeled away. Just as he was about to release my hand, the top lock clicked. Romell looked at me and tightened his grip. I looked at the next lock. Watching the bolt disengage, I smacked my forehead at my own stupidity. Spider didn't only have one set of keys; he had two. I tried to tug my hand away from Romell's; he squeezed even tighter. Spider stuck his key in that third lock, and the friction was loud. My knees grew weak, and I felt like I was going to faint. Here I was, alone in my apartment with Romell, in my nightgown with no panties on. Now, Spider was unlocking the door, and Romell was squeezing my hand. The thumb turn on the bottom lock rotated, and my heart...my heart sank to my stomach. When I saw the knob twist, I closed my eyes and held my breath.

What Else to Try?

$\mathcal{S}$ PIDER WAS COMING IN, AND ROMELL WAS NOT letting go of my hand. I got strength from somewhere, snatching my hand away just before the heavy door swung all the way open. The first face Spider saw was Romell's. Spider did a double take, and then his eyes grew bigger than mine. I watched the blood drain from his face, fading his copper tan pale. My courage came back. I got bold and took control of the situation. I rolled my eyes. "What the hell are you doing here?"

"I came to talk to you," Spider said.

Now, I didn't know which way to turn. Spider was left. Romell was on my right. I turned right. Romell's lips were tight and twisted to the side. This was the first time these two had been in the same room since high school. Now, they were men. Two bodies towered over me like skyscrapers, both drenched. Romell stood tall in his t-shirt and jeans; Spider, a little taller in yesterday's suit. But, despite all Spider's layers, Romell's upper body had more bulk. Spider was long and lean, but built like a strip of bacon compared to Romell.

Romell's velvety voice went way deep. "Mr. Snyder," he said. Then, he looked back and forth at both of us and said, "Miss Love?" The way he said it confused me. The inflection in his voice left me wondering whether he was asking Spider if he missed me or asking me what I was going to do. I froze because I didn't know what to say or do or what

Romell would do next. Frozen, I watched Romell moisten *his* lips and lean toward mine. My quick reflexes kicked in. I snapped my head to the side, and he kissed me on my right cheek. Then, with a smirk, he looked Spider up and down and brushed past him. From the hall, he looked back. "Mia, I'll be seeing you."

I looked at him; he was squinting into my eyes and nodding. So I knew he was going to wait for me.

I nodded back. "Okay, Romell."

Then, Spider spoke. "Hey, Romell! I'll catch you later."

Romell squinted at Spider, then simultaneously, both Spider and Romell snapped back their heads. Romell looked at Spider for a moment and then casually swaggered off.

I locked the door and looked at Spider. His expression was blank. That was not good. Now, I had no clue what he was thinking, no indication of how he would react, and no idea what I should do to handle the situation. There was another problem; Spider wanted to talk, but I couldn't remember how Romell left that bedroom. So whatever Spider wanted to talk about, I had to make sure this exchange happened in the living room.

I grabbed onto Spider's damp sleeve and pulled him over to the loveseat. He snatched out of my grasp and started up the hall. I grabbed him again. He yanked away. "What's up with you? I have to use the bathroom."

"Oh, okay," I said. *So much for that.* I watched Spider walk into the bathroom. Then, I took off to the bedroom.

Hearing Spider use the toilet, I looked around fast. The sheets were rumpled. Smoothing them out, I felt a damp patch at the foot of the bed. The toilet flushed, and then the faucet ran. There was no time to change the sheets. I snatched the pillow off the floor and covered the spot. As I went to stand back up, I caught a glimpse of the foiled wrapper under the crib. Quickly, I knelt, snatched it into my hand and crumpled it up. I was just about to pitch it into the wastebasket when Spider walked in. So, instead, I tightened my fist and sat on the side of the bed, hoping that Spider didn't notice how hard I was breathing. Then, I eased the bottom of my gown under my thigh so that he wouldn't notice I wasn't wearing underwear.

"What was Romell doing here?"

"He had something important to tell me." Spider looked at me. His eyes weren't satisfied, so I added, "He just lost his job."

"Is that all? Because, it looked like he was up to something."

"Why are you here? You want your clothes? Your money? What?"

"I wanna talk to you!"

"Well, talk. And, make it quick."

"What's the rush?"

"I just wanna get this over with."

"I wanna try to work things out," he said.

"Why?"

"Where am I going? We've always been a couple!"

"It's over, Spider!"

"Mia, I'm not done. I'm not just gonna let ten years go down the drain, just like that!"

"The past ten years were a waste of time, Spider!"

"A waste of time? What about our son?"

"What about my marriage proposal?" I said.

He walked over and knelt in front of me, placed his hand on my knee, and tried to kiss my neck. I pulled away, saying, "What are you doing?"

"What does it look like I'm doing?" His sad eyes sparkled in the light. They were red and so was his nose. I could tell he was crying. The only reason why I wasn't fazed was because Romell had just left. I clenched my right hand even tighter around the condom wrapper. Spider leaned in to kiss my lips. I turned my head, and he kissed me on the left cheek instead. *Spider looks good, but I am not going to revisit old feelings, and even if I wanted to, I'm not wearing any panties. Wait a minute. Where are my panties?* I casually glanced around, but I didn't see them. He looked into my eyes, and the next thing I knew, his hand started creeping up my thigh. I brushed it away, and Spider whined in frustration. "Stop playing around! I miss you."

"You missed out."

"You're still pissed off? Okay. Okay, I fucked up! I didn't mean to hurt your feelings or call you stupid! Now, can we get past this?"

Spider's admitting he's wrong. That's a first. But now, it's too little too late. We could've gotten past this if my night was different or Spider had been about an hour earlier. I shook my head. "Are you going to take your things with you now, or come back for them later?"

"Mia, why are you buggin' on me like this? This shit is minor. You want a proposal? Fine, I've got a ring in my pocket. I wanted to wait until I could do this right, but here you go. I wanna marry you!" He grabbed my left hand. For a moment, I forgot which hand the condom wrapper was in, but it was in my right. Spider took hold of my ring finger and slipped on a gold band. "That's my mother's old ring. Is that good enough for you?"

The gold was pinkish. I think they call it rose gold. The old band was embossed with a motif of flowers. I looked up at him. "Hell no! That ring is jinxed!"

Spider laughed. "Your ring is at the jeweler's."

"What ring?"

"I got you an engagement ring. It's being mounted at the jeweler's as we speak."

"What jeweler? Where?"

"You forget the Diamond District is right around the corner from my job."

I twisted my lips. "You did that this morning,

right?"

"No. I've had this ring on layaway for a year now. That's why I was bugging you about that résumé for so long, and that's also why I got the computer for you to type it on. I needed money to pay for the ring. I just got a promotion, but the label's only been giving me a stipend for carfare and lunch. So, all I could do was five or ten dollars here and there, and on the days I brought lunch in, I put five more on it."

"Yeah, right! Spider, I asked you the other day when we were going to get married, and you said eventually. You were *not* making payments on a ring!"

"I promised you we'd get married after Tee-Bo was born," he said, reaching into his pocket and pulling out a bunch of yellow receipts that were stapled together. He then handed them to me. There were a lot of payments written in, but the date on the top copy was August 4th, the day after I told him I was pregnant.

Spider looked at me. "A promise is a promise," he whispered. "Moments like this happen once in a lifetime, so I always wanted to do this right. Pop the question the old-fashioned way so I could always remember the look on your face. And, I knew if I skimped on the ring, your sister would never let you live it down. So, I picked out the nicest ring I could find. That's why I told you we would get married eventually. Making five-dollar payments, it would've taken me forever to pay for it. But, since I got the insurance check, I paid it off two days ago. I'm supposed to pick it up tomorrow."

I closed my eyes. Tears stung for a few reasons. One, I had no idea. Had I known, I would've made the effort to do his résumé, and I definitely would've been more patient. Two, there was no way I could accept this. If I did, Spider would definitely want some sex, and I was sitting here with no panties on. And three, I had waited so long for him to propose to me. And now he finally did, but Romell was downstairs waiting to take me back to *his* house. I was at a complete loss for words, so I opened my mouth and said what I was thinking, "Spider, why didn't you tell me you were making payments on an engagement ring?"

"Tell you? 'Aye, Mia. I got a down payment on an engagement ring, so when I pop the question, be sure to act surprised.' Doesn't that seem a little foolish to you?"

I sighed, looked at the antique wedding band on my finger, and changed the subject. "So, everything is okay with you and Dr. Snyder?"

He shook his head. "She gave me that ring a while ago."

"I guess she *is* pretty good at keeping secrets," I mumbled.

He didn't respond to that. I don't think he heard me. He took a deep breath, and said, "You know, for a very long time I resented Pops because I felt my mother was the victim in that situation. She had me feeling it was my place to right the wrongs in their relationship by living my life perfectly. But, that's not possible. I'm human!"

"We *all* are human."

He shrugged. "I just wish she could've been straight with me."

I wanted to say, *No, you wish she could've been straight.* What his mother did in the privacy of her bedroom was her own personal business. Even as uncomfortable as I was about homosexuality, had that been my mother, her being in love with a woman really wouldn't matter. I looked at Spider. His eyes were glossy. He was about to cry. His lips were parted. I waited for him to say something, even though the silence was getting stale. Eventually, he looked at me and said, "My mother told me where I can find Pop's ashes. Right now, that's all I care about. Enough about that, what day do you wanna make it official?"

I looked away. "I need to think about this."

"What's there to think about?"

"How can a marriage between us work when you don't appreciate me? You can't even tell me you love me!"

"Just because I didn't say it, doesn't mean I didn't feel it! Cause believe me, I had to appreciate your ass a whole lot to think I was going to pay for a ten thousand dollar ring five dollars at a time."

I blinked and quickly recovered, "Why wait until now to say so! If you care so much about me, why didn't you tell me before? What took you so...damn...long?"

He didn't say anything.

I shook my head. "Just as I thought, you don't love me. You just want to hold on to me the way you hold on to everything else, but I'm not going to be another relic from your past." I wrapped my fingers tightly around the ring and pulled it off.

"Mia, wait," he said. "I was afraid, okay."

"Afraid of what?"

He walked to the corner by the door and looked over. "You and your boy are so close, I was always afraid you'd wake up one morning and decide he's the one you want to be with. So, I held back. That way, if things ever did jump off between you two, it wouldn't hurt as bad."

"So, let me get this straight; you were holding back because you were afraid you were going to lose me?"

"Yeah, but I almost lost you anyway, because I was holding back." He laughed and said, "Kind of ironic, huh?"

I sighed and shook my head. "I love you, Spider, and you don't have to worry about me. I won't let anyone or anything come between us." I tried to put the ring back on but it slipped out of my fingers, hit the crib's rail and rolled under the bed.

He smiled and started toward me. Then, he knelt down and stopped short. He looked at me. "What's that?" he said.

"What's what?"

"Underneath the bed. Are those…your panties?"

We Go Through the Motions...

I WANTED SO BADLY TO GET TO THOSE PANTIES first; that way, I could scrunch them into a ball and pretend they were laundry. But, Spider got to them before I could. He held up my ripped panties, but I guess part of him couldn't accept what he saw. He still felt the need to snatch my gown up and look at my naked ass with his own two eyes. Part of me wanted to stand my ground. Another part of me wanted to run, scream, and hide. And, still another part of me wanted to smack him and hightail it out of there. Somehow, there was a part of me that believed I could explain my way out of this. "Spider, it's not what you think."

"Don't lie to me." His voice was angry and quiet. "How long, Mia?"

"We didn't do anything. Let me explain."

"How long!"

"Only this one time. And, it's not like you and I were together."

"We broke up yesterday!" He sat on the edge of the bed and dropped his head into his hands. Then, he started laughing. "Ain't this about a bitch! *I'm* a lying, no good, cheating, dirty dog, huh?" He looked back at me smiling, but it wasn't a natural smile. It was more like he was baring his fangs. I could see anguish burning in his eyes, but I could only respond by silently shaking my head. "You've got more self-control than anybody, huh?" Now, I could only respond by dropping my head. Spider jumped up. He paced, beating his forehead with the heel of his hand for a while, before he looked at me and screamed, "Damn! Couldn't you at least let the bed get cold?" He took a deep breath. This time he inhaled through his nose and exhaled through his mouth in a way that made his lips expand. Our prom picture was still lying facedown. He picked it up, looking at it. He motioned like he was about to throw it across the room but stopped himself and sat it upright on the dresser. "I can't say I didn't expect this. Now, get dressed and let's go," he said.

"Let's go where?"

"The Justice of the Peace is up on the Concourse. We can take a walk over there, make it official, now, and then have some kind of ceremony for our families later."

"I'm sorry, I can't."

"What do you mean you can't? You can if you want to!"

"I don't know what I want right now."

"Do you want to get married or don't you?"

"No."

"What are you saying?"

"I'm saying, no. No, Spider. No."

"You wanna be with your boy?"

"I don't know."

He jumped up and knocked everything off the dresser. "Ten years, Mia! That fucking means nothing to you?"

By now, my tears were flowing. "It does, Spider. But—"

"But what!"

"I've known Romell all my life."

"You wanna be with your boy, Mia? You wanna be with your boy! Go right ahead!" He took his keys out of his pocket and threw them into my bedroom mirror. They hit the frame and the mirror shifted.

"Spider, don't do that! You're gonna break something!"

He bit his lip and looked at me with tears in his eyes. "Break something? Break something! You broke my fucking heart, Mia! You broke my heart."

Spider sat on the corner of the bed, covered his face, and broke into heavy sobs. I came over to him and he jumped up, screaming, "Don't touch me!" He then walked out of the room and down the hall.

I sat there on my bed, waiting for the front door to slam. It didn't. Spider's wind up clock ticked, ticked, and ticked. I hopped off the bed, slipped on my slippers, and listened. Nothing. I ran to my bedroom door and placed my hand on the doorknob. Then, I heard a series of booms and then, the shatter of breaking glass and Spider's ear-piercing scream.

And Pretend...

HEN I REACHED THE OTHER END OF THE HALL, my heavy mirror was facedown, and Spider was standing over my loveseat, shaking his right hand violently. The back of that hand was sliced open. Skin was just hanging. Blood was spurting, running down his arm, and dripping all over the place. Trying not to panic, I said, "I'll get you a towel."

Spider looked like he was about to bleed to death, but that didn't stop him from hollering, "Stay the fuck away from me!" He pulled his red tie out of his back pocket and wrapped it tightly around his hand. Then, he walked to the door, yanking it open so hard the knob left a dent in the wall. Just before he walked out, he screamed, "Bitches ain't shit!"

Blood was all over my loveseat. I could clearly see half a handprint on the arm. My living room—my poor living room—had broken glass scattered from one end to the other. His computer was on the floor sideways. My blue vase was on the floor, shattered. There was so much glass I didn't know what to do or where to begin. Where the mirror once hung, a patch in the wall was stripped down to what looked like cardboard. I lifted my mirror back off the chest. The glass was broken. Blood was covering the pieces. It looked like my seven-year run of bad luck had already started. I stepped carefully over to the door. I looked out into the corridor. There was blood on the floor, but Spider was nowhere to be seen. As soon as

I locked the door, my phone rang.

"Chocolate, are you okay?"

I burst into tears. "Spider just left!"

"I saw him! What happened?"

"Spider saw my ripped panties on the floor and went ballistic!"

"What the fuck happened!"

"He trashed my place! He cut his hand and walked out, calling me all kinds of bitches!"

"Oh!" I heard Romell exhale and then he chuckled. After that, he said, "He cut *his own* self. In that case, come on down, Chocolate. Let's go."

"I've got to do something about this room! There's blood and glass everywhere!"

"Don't even worry about that now. No harm done. Whatever he damaged, we can always replace. Take a ride with me downtown, and I'll help you clean up that mess when we get back."

"No! You go on, Romell. I...I need time...I need to clear my head. When I'm ready to talk, I'll call you."

"Are we gonna talk about us?"

"What us? There is no *us*."

"You've got to be kidding me! Listen, Chocolate! I'm begging you. Please, don't do this now."

"You don't even want me, Romell!"

"I want you more than I've ever wanted anything!"

"You didn't last night."

"I did, Chocolate!"

"You threw me out!"

"You weren't thinking straight, and I care too much to take advantage of you like that."

"You care too much? You care too much about *me*?"

"Yeah, last night, you were acting out, because you broke up with your man; all along, I knew he was coming back, so I didn't want to take advantage of the situation."

"So, last night you didn't sleep with me, because you knew Spider was coming back?"

"Yeah."

"And you didn't want to take advantage of the situation?"

"Yeah!"

"Today, you still *knew* Spider was coming back. So, you *were* trying to take advantage!"

"No, Mia! That's not what I was doing!"

"Then, what do you call it?"

He didn't answer.

"Romell, you play too many games."

"You want me to be honest with you?"

"Yes!"

"Okay! I saw an opportunity, and I jumped on it! That's the real! Last night, I wanted some ass, but that's all I wanted, Mia. You and I can't be fuck buddies! I learned *that* when you slapped me earlier. If I'm gonna be with *you*, I have to be ready to step up and be what you need. I didn't know if I could do that last night, but this morning, a gut feeling told me it was now or never. So, I spent half the morning parked right here in front of your building. First, I was just sitting in my car, checking for your man. Then, I was trying to make up my mind about whether to come up or not. And then, I was trying to figure out how I was gonna pitch it to you; because I knew I was gonna hear your mouth. I was so preoccupied with finding just the right words to say that a raggedy-ass, garbage truck came by and scratched the fucking paint off my Jaguar. But did I get upset? No, I locked my car and went to get change for a dollar...in dimes. This ain't a game to me, Chocolate. And I'll keep it real with you. Your ass ain't perfect! You're bossy, you're loud, and you got a fucked up attitude sometimes. But then again, sometimes you're the sweetest, most beautiful person I know. I love the way I feel when I'm around you. You're my heart, Chocolate. You! I could have anybody. I could have everybody! But I'd rather be with you, because no one else makes me feel this way. And I'll keep it really real. We ain't even fuckin' yet!"

"Do you really mean that? Or are you just telling me what you think I want to hear?"

Sounding as if he'd stopped just short of crying, he answered, "This ain't game! I wouldn't even be here if I wasn't dead-ass serious! I wanna be with you! I'll do whatever it takes! You and I will be *so* happy together!"

I wanted so badly to believe him. I squeezed my eyes tight. There were no tears, but I was one big bubble of angst. All I knew was that I wanted this feeling to stop. "What makes you so sure we'll be happy?"

"We're happy now!"

"Romell, there's glass and blood...all over my living room. *I'm* not happy right now!"

He laughed. "Okay, okay. I'll come up and help you clean that mess *before* we go."

"Romell! The man I've loved for the past ten years just crumbled right before my eyes."

"He'll recover."

"Romell! You don't get it! I can't! I can't do this. I can't be with you."

"You're gonna choose him over *me*?"

"No, I'm leaving you both alone."

"Fuck that! I'm coming up!" When I heard Romell say that, I slammed the phone down. It rang immediately, and I picked up only to hear Romell scream, "I'm coming up!"

"Don't you dare!" I slammed the phone down again.

Romell called back again. "You can't stop me!"

"Romell, if you show up at my door, I will spit in your face! I *don't* want to see you!"

I hung up again, but this time, I pulled the cord out of the phone. Making my way across the room, glass crunched beneath the soles of my slippers, even though I tried to avoid the bigger pieces. Once at the window, I sat on the radiator and looked out at Romell's black Jaguar. I didn't know if Romell would come up or go on home, and if he came up, I didn't know what I'd do. Because, no matter what I said, I would never spit at Romell. That's nasty.

Outside in front of the building, Romell stepped out of his car and shut the door. He walked halfway to the entrance, and then he turned around. The next thing I knew Romell tore out of his parking spot and took off down the street like it wasn't even raining. I don't know if he saw the stop sign at the corner or not, but he went straight through it. From my window, I watched his black Jag and a minivan collide at the intersection. The airbag deployed and the front end of his car crumpled like paper. He got out of the car and I could see his arms flailing as he argued with the other driver out in that heavy rain. But not only did Romell have the stop sign, he was driving too damn fast. He banged on his hood, climbed back in the car, and shut the door. Not too long after that I heard the bedroom phone ring. I grabbed the phone off my loveseat and pushed the wire back into the base. "What?"

"Chocolate, I need to come up."

"No."

"I was just in an accident!"

"You have a cell phone!"

"You're gonna leave *me* standing out here in the rain?"

"Good-bye, Romell."

"Oh, wow. You're really gonna do me like that?"

"I said good-bye, didn't I? Yes, I am being a bitch! At this point, I don't care if I'm being a bitch! I really don't care! Spider already called me all kinds of bitches! So you can go right ahead and call me all kinds of bitches, too. Go ahead, Romell! I know you want to!"

"Nah. My mom raised me right. I would never stoop so low as to call any woman a dog. But I will say this: how could any man love and respect you if you don't love and respect yourself? Good-bye, Mia. It was nice knowing you."

Is This The Beginning of The End?

I SAT IN THE WINDOW AND WATCHED ROMELL PUSH his car out of the intersection over to the curb. He then sat back inside and waited. I watched, but Romell's words hurt my heart. No, it was his tone. Normally, Romell didn't speak; he purred, and when he was upset, he'd yell and scream. That meant, on some level, he cared. Now, more so than his words, it was his tone that told me our friendship was over. He didn't argue anymore. His anger took him to a place where he had emotionally disengaged. Now, he was cordial.

This may have been hard for him to understand, but I'd had it. I wasn't allowing anyone to pressure me to do anything anymore. If I spent my life trying to make everyone else happy, I'd go crazy. Still, this is not the way I wanted things to turn out. I never wanted to hurt Romell. He'd been my best friend forever. I loved spending time with him. He was the one I was most comfortable talking to. He was drawn to pretty faces, so he never noticed mine; that *did* bother me. I'm a black woman; he didn't date black women. I had a serious problem with that, but I never wanted to see Romell hurt. I never wanted to hurt Spider, either. I always wanted to be the best thing that ever happened to Spider. I tried so hard to be everything he needed just so Spider would know he'd never find another woman like me. There were times I felt unloved, and there were definitely times when I felt unappreciated, but I never ever wanted to break Spider's heart.

A big red tow truck pulled up in front of the Jaguar and Romell stepped out of his car into the rain. While the tow truck hooked and hoisted his Jag, Romell stood on the sidewalk with his hand in his pocket and his posture bent. Even from my window, I could see he was sulking. I shrugged. *No matter what I decided, someone I cared about would've been hurt. That's why I didn't plan any of this. I had a crush on Romell a very long time ago. Now, I know Romell and I sort of had sex, but that would never have happened if Spider and I didn't break up. That is the only reason why I let my guard down.*

This is all Spider's fault. Spider should've told me he was paying on a ring. If he did, we would be together right now. But instead, his ass had me bending over backwards thinking I wasn't good enough to marry, and all along, he had the damn ring on layaway. Spider was broke. How was I supposed to know he had a ring on layaway? Then again, prom night, Spider gave me a ring. He saved up the money from his part-time job. He took me to the movies two weeks later. I went to the ladies room and took it off to wash my hands. That was the last I saw of it, but he did buy me a ring then, I should've known he'd buy me a ring now. It was understood that we'd eventually get married, but without a set date, to me eventually meant never. Bottom line is I can't blame Spider. We both agreed to cut our friends off. But, I didn't. Instead of typing Spider's proposal, I emailed that poem to Romell. Then, I went to see him. And, it's because of that "Chocolate Love" poem that Romell decided to cross the line. Just like I wanted my marriage proposal, Spider wanted his marketing proposal. And, if I would've just typed Spider's proposal like I was supposed to, none of this would've happened. I could've done that at any time, but I didn't. So how can I blame Spider? I sighed. *Shoulda-woulda-couldas never did a bit of good. I guess at this point, it doesn't matter whose fault it is; I can't change the past. I've just got to find a way to fix this situation now.*

The damaged front end of Romell's car was now completely elevated. He walked around to the passenger side of the truck and climbed into the cab. They pulled off. I didn't know what garage they were taking it to, but to me, the Jag looked totaled. I shook my head. *How can I fix this situation? Maybe the situation doesn't need fixing. Who knows? Maybe Spider and I can still be together. It was always supposed to be just the three of us—me, Spider, and Tee-Bo. We weren't supposed to let anyone or anything get in the way of that. Maybe I should just page Spider and tell him I changed my mind. It wasn't like me and Romell actually had sex; we almost did. And, it's not like I felt anything deep for Romell outside of my feelings for him as a friend.*

By now, my ass was numb, and pins and needles were radiating down to my toes. I stepped off the radiator, shaking out my leg and looked around at all the glass in my living room. *My work is definitely cut out for me here. I don't even know where to start. Compared to today, last night was fun and games. And last night I wanted to kill myself. Now, I know suicide is not an option. It's a good thing I already realized that or I would not have been able to deal with all this.* I sighed. *I'm going to put my house back in order. And when I'm done, I'll page Spider. As soon as he calls, I'm going to tell him I've changed my mind. We will get married like we're supposed to, and we'll be a family, just the three of us.*

Stepping around glass, I made my way to the kitchen, and got the broom. I tied a plastic bag around the bristles, slung a heavy-duty trash bag over my arm, and dropped the condom wrapper into it. I dragged the plastic covered bristles across the floor, and shards of glass scratched the wood. *I'm doing this for the three of us.* I reminded myself. Sitting the broom down, I moved the empty silver frame and carefully placed a foot-long shard in the plastic bag. And another. The third piece sliced my fingertip. It hurt like hell, but when I wiped the blood away and examined it, it was just a scratch, only about the size of a paper cut. I should have worn rubber gloves for this. I made my way to the medicine cabinet, and then into my bedroom.

I was trying to get through cleaning this mess by focusing on us three being a family again. Now, I had cut my finger. I needed a moment to regroup. I knelt near the bed and slipped my hand between the mattress and box spring for my poetry journal, but felt the cold metal of my silver bracelet. I pulled it out, fastened it on my arm and then retrieved my journal.

The ribbon bookmark was at my last poem, *I Just Can't Believe.* I turned the page back to *Is This the Beginning of the End* and read the last lines.

> *4 some reason*
> *4 some cause*
> *4 some strange reason*
> *It's just not obvious*
>
> *Please show me*
> *What I don't see*
> *What's the reason?*
> *4 the problem*

I tilted my head, looking at the words, *4 some reason. What's the reason? 4 the problem. For;* I consistently substituted that word with the number 4.

And, the funny thing is, I don't know why I did that. Was there any significance? Or was it just a mindless omission? I don't remember. There's me, Spider, and Tee-Bo—us three. There is no connection, unless Mommy or Dawn is the fourth element. Maybe I'm looking too much into this. Sitting with my legs crossed Indian style, I rested my head in both hands, thinking. *I am looking too deeply into this. Four could mean anything. We live on the fourth floor. The Fourth of July is right around the corner.* I looked at Dr. Snyder's antique wedding band on my left ring finger. Then the bracelet on my right wrist glimmered in the light. I read the inscription. *4 Ever Love Romell.* The "for" in forever was replaced with the number four. My conscience read those words as a question. *Four; ever love Romell?* Now, I had to honestly ask myself. *Did I ever love Romell?* First my nose stung, then my eyes started tearing. *I always loved Romell.* There was no use in denying it anymore. I was in love with Romell; for that reason, he was that fourth element. Romell was the problem. So, I couldn't consider getting back together with Spider now or ever.

I can't fix this. This is a mess. My life is a mess. For so long, I hoped to marry Spider and dreamed of being with Romell. It never dawned on me that my hopes and dreams were in opposition. Today is the day they all seem to come true. Now what? I sighed. *Why couldn't Romell just notice me in the ninth grade before I met Spider? If only Spider had told me he put the ring on layaway, then I wouldn't have....*I sighed. For so long, I'd envisioned Spider dropping down on one knee and slipping a large diamond on my finger. In my heart, I believed that would happen, until everyone else had me thinking otherwise. Now, not only did Spider propose, but he was also remorseful and appreciative. I saw with my own eyes how much Spider loved me when he realized Romell and I had sex. Instead of getting pissed off, he panicked and wanted to marry me right away. As for Romell, he never noticed me before; now, he noticed me. Romell didn't date black women; now, he wanted *me*. And, Romell never wanted a relationship ever; *now*, he wanted me. *Why did all of this have to happen now? Now, things will never be what they used to be. Why couldn't things just work out the way I planned? Why does love have to be so difficult?* I agonized over those thoughts until I remembered what Mrs. Goodwin said, "Love as we understand it, changes. God's love doesn't change." That was a concept I could only partially grasp. I understood about love, but I needed to find out about God.

I opened my night table and pulled out my Bible. Spider's wad of cash lay in a rubber band in the drawer. I closed it and opened the Bible at random. The first verse I saw caught my attention. "Therefore I tell you, whatever you ask for in prayer, believe that you have received it, and it will be yours." (Mark 11:24). I closed the Bible and smiled. *Mrs. Goodwin said, she's been praying for me. I believe that. I'm so glad someone was praying for me when I wasn't even praying for myself. That has to be the reason why I'm still here.* I grabbed my journal and turned to my last poem, *I Just Can't Believe.* I snatched it out and tore it up. Now, there was something I absolutely had to do.

I got down on my knees, clasped my hands together tightly, and closed my eyes. But I was afraid. I was too afraid to pray for anything specific, so I said the only prayer that came to mind, *The Lord's Prayer.* Over and over, I don't know how many times. My fists were clenched so tightly; my hands began to sweat. When I was done, I stretched the cramps out of my fingers, wiped tears from my eyes, and thought for a moment. *Mrs. Goodwin said living in the world unsure about your beliefs is like the love of your life and your soul mate being two different people. I couldn't relate to that before. Oh boy, did I understand that now.*

I wanted to call Mrs. Goodwin back, but I didn't want her to think I was calling because I wanted to go to church with her. I looked out the window. I needed a life preserver to go out in that rain. It was too bad out there to go anywhere, but there was still something I needed to ask Mrs. Goodwin. I took a deep breath. *I'll just make this conversation quick.* I picked up the phone and dialed her at work. She answered, "Fort Apache Outreach. Margaret Goodwin speaking."

"Hi, Mrs. Goodwin."

"Hello, Mia. What's wrong?"

"Nothing. I'm just curious. What do you do when the love of your life and your soul mate *are* two different people?"

"You make a choice."

That wasn't the response I was looking for. "Oh, okay. I'll talk to you later."

"Is that all?" she asked.

"Why?"

"I thought you were calling to let me know you're coming to service."

"No way." I looked out the window into the pouring rain. "Not in this weather."

"Okay, dear. I'll be talking to you."

I hung up, thinking. *Make a choice. How? There's only one choice I can make. This will probably be the hardest thing I've ever done, but I gotta do what I gotta do.* I removed the silver link bracelet and placed it in my night table drawer. As soon as I could get to a Post Office, that would be mailed back to Romell. I then pulled the wedding band off my ring finger. I placed it in the drawer atop Spider's wad of cash. As soon as he came back for his things, I would give him back his ring and his money.

Now, I need to find the strength to move on. I'm weak, so I know I'll need some help with this. Maybe

Dawn could keep me in check with this one. If Dawn checks up on me, that would definitely help. Dawn said, realizing I need help is not a sign of weakness; it's a sign of strength. She said I need Jesus. Well, I prayed so I'm good. I sighed. Okay. I do need Jesus, but it's a mess out there. So, I am not going to church in the rain. And, only churchy people go to church in the middle of the week, anyway; I am not a churchy person. So, I am not going, I'm not. Not today. Not in this weather. No way.

♥ ♥ ♥ ♥

Reverend Earl and old Deacon Thomas were standing at the head of the church. Deacon Thomas cleared his throat, and said, "Praise Him! Praise Him!" Then he bowed his head and sang the same prayer he always sang at this part of the service. *"Heavenly, Father, we are gathered here in this sanctuary today, and we want to say thank You! Thank you for waking us up this morning...in our right minds. For giving us life! And strength! You didn't have to do it, but You did. You are the Alpha...the Omega...the beginning, and the end. Father, I thank You that through You, all things are possible. All things! We humbly ask for Your continued guidance and protection this day and every day...in Jesus' name we pray. Let the church say, Amen! If there is anyone here in the middle of a crisis, I want you to know that God is the solution. If you feel it in your heart right now, come to Jesus...."*

I felt numb, but a hand touched my shoulder. I looked up into Mrs. Goodwin's smiling, brown face and saw Romell's eyes and dimples. "Hi," I whispered and scooted over, making room for her full figure. Then, I looked again at Deacon Thomas.

He clapped his hands. *"Jesus is the only one who can be everything you need! He'll take your broken pieces, fix you up, and make you new...."*

Mrs. Goodwin gave me a squeeze. She crossed her long, thick legs, fanning herself with a stick fan of Dr.

King that was probably older than me. "I knew you'd be here today," she whispered.

I was puzzled. "How? I told you there was no way I was coming."

Still smiling, she said, "God makes a way."

I smiled back, wiping away the tear that escaped.

"Does anyone here want to come to Jesus today?"

I looked around at the handful of people scattered through-out the church. No one moved. I then stood and squeezed by Mrs. Goodwin. My legs wobbled, walking down the aisle toward Reverend Earl and Deacon Thomas, but when I stopped at the altar, I stood firm and said, "I do."

I had always thought I'd say those words with Spider standing next to me. I had hoped at that time we'd be *here*. Knowing how unlikely it was for Spider to marry me in a church, I would've settled for the Justice of the Peace. But why should I settle? Neither Spider nor Romell were in any position to love me the way I deserved to be loved. And as different as they were, the one thing they had in common was that they both felt entitled to whatever they wanted, regardless of what anyone else had to say about it. If they could feel entitled, why shouldn't I? I had just as much right to my happiness as everyone else. Mrs. Goodwin said if I put God first, everything else would fall into place. So standing here now, I was more hopeful than ever. In fact, I made up my mind. One day I would stand at this altar again. When that day came, I'd know that the man standing next to me would be the right man for me. Who that is exactly, only time will tell.

BONUS
No More Goodwin, Livings, & Moore

Romell Goodwin is a young, aspiring, Wall Street executive. He is talented and overconfident, but despite his intelligence and incredible drive, opportunities elude him. No More Goodwin, Livings & Moore is the tale of how he comes to realize that workplace politics are never fair. **This selection was first published in LOVING BLACK MEN: An Anthology released from Castle Black Publishing, edited by Mel and Christopher Bynum. This selection is also published in the GRAFFITI MURAL Collection.**

My last day at Livings & Moore began just like any other day. I walked into the office suite, and as usual, the first person I saw was leggy, Kathy Barker. Immediately left of the doorway, hers were bare and crossed at the knee. Bouncing her foot drew attention to her thighs. I acknowledged Kathy by nodding in her direction, but ignored her when she winked back. Coffee was already brewing. Dark roast was in the air. "Good morning, Mr. Goodwin. You're looking handsome as ever." Kathy's very high, open-toe shoes stepped from around the reception counter over to the Espresso machine. She started as a temp with three responsibilities: answer phones, make copies, and bring coffee. Her message taking was so bad, we automated the system, and everyone now resorted to making their own copies. It was definitely Kathy's breast job that transformed an office of men into caffeine addicts. The few times I had her coffee, there were grounds floating in it. It was like I was drinking dirt. Still, Kathy won herself a permanent position with benefits. As usual, her dress was a second skin. Judging by the length of it, she was looking for a raise.

"Good morning, Miss Barker. None for me today, but thanks." Somehow, I always knew she was setting a trap for someone. It wouldn't be this homeboy. Instinctively, I stayed away.

"I'm starting to feel unappreciated," she said.

I kept my head and my face straight when I answered, "Don't. Everyone else loves your coffee."

As I walked through the aisles, I passed newspapers, half-eaten bagels, and cups of Kathy's fuel. For the longest time, I was always here first. Somehow my work ethic had changed the dynamic. These days, half the firm was eager enough to show up more than an hour early. A leaning stack of reports was waiting on my desk. I walked up, took off my blazer, and hung it on the edge of my cubicle. Then, I laid my newspaper down and pulled my HP out of my briefcase. On top of the reports was a lone sheet of paper. I chucked it into the in-tray and sat. In this business, information is crucial. My mind was already in process mode. I grabbed one of those second-quarter reports and flipped through it.

Anyone who paid attention knew I was not one for small talk. But, there's always one. "Hey, Romell. What's happening? Those are some bad-ass shoes, my man."

That was Ian Sharpe. My loafers were Bruno Maglis. They were stylish, I'll give him that much. Had I been wearing goldfish platforms, an Afro, bell bottoms, and a Dashiki, maybe I would've slapped him five on the black-hand side and we both could've done the Boogaloo to Wild Cherry. But this was 1995 and this white boy was sounding like a pimp plucked from a blaxploitation flick. I knew these guys here considered me a threat, because I was young, only twenty-five years old, and hungry. I was the only brother in Livings & Moore to make it out of the mailroom, because I asked "too many questions" about our employee stock options. I have dark skin and the bald head. My height and athletic build would be considered physically imposing, were it not for the fact that I happen to be so incredibly good looking. Realizing I'm a presence, I'd come to work dressed better than most, first in Armani and now, custom tailored. Ian still felt it necessary to approach me with slick jive talk. I didn't teach (ESL) Ebonics as a Second Language. I was the senior analyst that trained him. We were the same age, but I had much more time vested with the company, because I completed undergrad in two and a half years. I lost all respect for the guy when I learned he was a mediocre ivy leaguer, whose daddy had the wherewithal to pull strings to get him in here, but thanks to me, Ian passed the exam. Now, he'd been licensed long enough to start figuring shit out on his own. Still he always seemed to find his way over to pester me when I had a ton of work to do, making every day a struggle not to punch him in the mouth.

When I didn't look up from my report, I guess he took it to mean I didn't hear him. He spoke louder. "Hey, my main man, I was searching through the firm's network, trying to locate that spreadsheet of yours, and I couldn't find it."

"You won't."

"Why not?"

"I developed those formulas. Those are my calculations. All my files are encrypted with a password and not backed up to the server. Any more questions?"

"How did you come up with something that complex?"

"I know what I'm doing."

"You must really have a high IQ."

"Nah, Ian. Mensa accepts retards. Now, if you don't mind," I pointed to the stack of the reports sitting on my desk and shooed him away with a hand gesture.

"Okay, just so you know. I picked you for my team. I'm sending an email with the details. I look forward to working together, man."

Ian left my cubicle just as Nick was walking by. Nick's a white boy, but his mother's Korean, and so is his wife for that matter. The first time I saw him, he seemed unusual and I couldn't pinpoint why. He's of average build and wore the standard blue suit, pale blue shirt, red tie, and Oxfords, just like every white boy in here. He's got the thick dark straight hair, darker skin, and eye shape that hinted at something. I found myself staring trying to figure out what that was, but I couldn't tell Nick was part Asian until I saw him standing with his wife. Nick was one of the coolest cats in the office, a pompous go-getter, but a straight shooter. Maybe, that's why we clicked. I smiled at Nick, shook my head, and said, "Good morning."

He walked over and sat, "You're taking this a lot better than I expected."

"Of course I am. I just roll with it. I don't let anything bother me," I said, but when I saw the shock in his expression, it occurred to me to ask, "What exactly do you mean?"

"Ian's promotion."

"Ian's promotion to what?"

He leaned in and whispered, "They're launching a major hedge fund. Ian was chosen to head up the technology division. That's the memo right there. Didn't you read it?"

I jumped up, and snatched the sheet out of my tray. Just like Nick said, it was announcing Ian's promotion. I paced for about a minute. Then, I marched over to Stevenson's office and knocked on his big mahogany door. When he said the word, I entered.

Stevenson looked up from his daily planner. The buttons on his blue dress shirt struggled to stay closed, while his undershirt played peek-a-boo. "What can I do for you, Romell?"

Standing in front of him, I said, "Mr. Stevenson, I have some concerns. I'd like to know exactly when I can expect my promotion."

"That's a little forward. Don't you think?"

"Maybe, but it seems to me this firm is handing out promotions like candy. If so, I'd like mine now."

"I take it you've read the memo."

I wanted to say: Fuck a memo! Somebody at this firm is purposely trying to fuck with me! But, I smiled and said, "Yes, Mr. Stevenson, sir. I've read the announcement. The fact that you guys gave away a position, that rightfully should have been mine, lets me know that no one here appreciates all the effort I'm putting in."

"That appointment was a decision of the board. It was not my doing. My advice to you is to just hang in there and try to make the best of it. In due time—"

"I've done my part!" I was extremely agitated, but I saw Stevenson reach for the intercom, probably to call security. I took a deep breath to calm myself and continued to object. "No. You're asking too much. I can't. I won't. In fact, I'd like to see how Ian's going to head up the tech division without my help."

"Why? Are you going somewhere?"

"Maybe. I have several offers." The truth was, I didn't want to work anywhere else. I was hoping I could move through the ranks here at Livings & Moore, until this place changed its name. Goodwin, Livings & Moore always did seem to have a nice ring to it.

Stevenson folded his hands and sat them on his gut. "Several offers, eh?"

"Big ones." Right then, I thought about my friend, Mia, and how she was trying to convince me to circulate my résumé and give the higher ups my list of demands and an ultimatum. Promote me or else. To me, all that was just tough talk from someone working for peanuts. I did not say what I said because I was following her advice. The money I was making was enough to appease me. I said what I said, because I had backed myself into a corner and didn't know what else to say. I knew I had a good head on my shoulders, and besides that, I was just plain tired of kissing up, smiling when I was pissed off, not being able to talk back, all so these assholes would one day throw me a bone. In a perfect world, I would already have contacted some head hunters or at the very least had a Plan B. I would've had something better lined up. In that perfect world, I would've told that fat bastard just how fat he was.

"Well, Romell. Far be it from me to stand in the way of your progress. If you've received a competitive offer, it would be in your best interest to take it."

"I agree."

Stevenson now pressed the intercom. "Bonnie, Mr. Goodwin will be leaving us. Drop everything and draft his letter of resignation. Then, bring it to his desk for signature."

Bonnie's voice buzzed through the static. "I don't believe I heard you correctly, sir."

"Type up a letter of resignation for Romell and bring it to him to sign. That'll be all, Bonnie." Stevenson motioned toward the empty leather chair across from the massive desk that held leather accessories, framed photos of his smiling wife and kid, a pencil and pen set, a clock, business card holder, books and bookends, and paper weights but no papers. All that time I had been in his office, I didn't even realize I remained standing. "Have a seat, Romell, so that we can discuss your severance package. I'm sure we can come up with a practical solution," he said.

And after I sat, he got to the point immediately, "Now, since you are leaving us, what I propose is this...."

That was when I saw who he really was. The funny thing was I thought I had Stevenson's support. I was only patient for so long because he kept reassuring me that if I waited a little while longer, he would make things happen for me. After-the-next-quarter turned into after-the-New-Year and then, after-the-reorganization. Stevenson didn't seem cutthroat like the other partners. He seemed timid, without backbone. Whenever I'd pull his coattail to question him about my promotion, he'd smile and nervously make me another promise. "Just hang in there, and

I'll see what I can do for you." I trusted that. But, I now realize there are no allies in this business. I got a better severance package for transitioning "all my clients" to Ian's team. Maybe the plan all along was for them to jack me for my contacts.

I was slumped at my desk, when I felt a rub on my back. I lifted my head. Bonnie had made it over with the letter. She was a middle-aged blond who still had a decent figure. She had been the secretary for over twenty years even though she was probably sharper than half the guys on the floor. She was like a second mother. She placed the letter in front of me. I looked at the fancy linen paper. Bonnie removed her cat-eye bifocals and rested them on her blouse. Her voice was soft but stern. "You don't have to do this. Don't let him force your hand."

"Why waste more time?"

Now she leaned down and whispered. "A friend of mine is an employee rights attorney. You'd have a pretty strong discrimination case. Fight this."

I knew I could fight it, but if I called myself trying to battle it out with Livings & Moore in court, my name wouldn't mean shit on Wall Street. Where else would I go? I shook my head and said, "Thanks, but no thanks. Can I borrow that pen?"

She sighed, pulled the felt-tipped pen from behind her ear, and as I signed the letter, she said, "I don't understand you."

"I know, but I'm gonna miss you, Mrs. Sutton." I handed her the letter and gave her a kiss on the cheek. Her blue eyes were glossy.

Stevenson's door was only a few feet away from my desk. Right before she entered his office with that letter, I overheard Bonnie say, "This breaks my heart."

Of course, my security escort came, a big, burly brother, looking like he was prepared to do someone some physical harm. By then, I had already ejected my computer's hard drive and swapped it for the blank one. I grabbed my stuff and headed to the door. As I passed Ian's desk, he was singing, "Another One Bites the Dust." I didn't lose my cool. Instead of continuing right on out though, I stopped, parked my box, and stepped to him. I then smiled and said, "Ian, this firm is full of sneaky, no talent, little dick mutherfuckers. You'll definitely fit in." After grabbing my nuts, I said, "Obviously, I don't." I then picked up my box and proceeded to the Exit. The security guard was no real threat. He looked at me, but didn't say a word. As he walked behind me, I heard him laughing to himself. And even though Ian's response to what I had said was to yell out, "Good riddance!" That didn't bother me. I had already said my piece.

LOVECHANGES
By Eartha Watts Hicks

Please take a moment and leave a Review.

All social media links

Facebook Personal:
https://www.facebook.com/earthatone

Facebook Fan:
https://www.facebook.com/earthawattshicks.lovech
anges

Amazon Author Page:
https://www.amazon.com/Eartha-Watts-
Hicks/e/B00HZV7ODS/ref=sr_ntt_srch_lnk_1?qid=1
483282323&sr=8-1

Twitter: @Earthatone

LinkedIn: https://www.linkedin.com/in/earthatone

Instagram: @Earthatone

Blogger: http://earthatone.blogspot.com/

Goodreads: https://www.goodreads.com/earthatone

Wattpad:
https://www.wattpad.com/user/EarthaWattsHicks

Pintrest: @Earthatone

SheWrites: @Earthatone

Also Available from Earthatone Books

Weaver by Miriam Kelly Ferguson

978-099148920-6

Graffiti Mural by Eartha Watts Hicks

978-099148923-7